I0545341

WAIT AND SEE

A Story of a Romance
and
Its Effects on Those Related

Wait and See

Edited by C.A. MacKenzie
Cover image courtesy of Scott Liddell
Cover design C.A. MacKenzie

ISBN-13: 978-1-927529-49-2
ISBN-10: 1927529492

MacKenzie Publishing
Halifax, Nova Scotia
September 2017
Second edition June 2018

Canadian/British spelling are used throughout.

MacKenzie Publishing

CONTENTS

PREFACE

When I first shared the draft of this story for feedback and advice, I told the helpers my two principal goals when writing this. I am advised these should be shared with the readers.

This story tries to describe the reactions and confusions of not just the two forty-somethings beginning an affair, but how it affects others to whom they are (or were) related.

I also played around with point of view. In almost all the chapters in parts one and two, the point of view switches from one character to another and then back to the original. If this switching annoys you, then you won't progress too far into the story.

When I began to look at how I could bring the novel to some sort of conclusion, I could not keep up this format—though I did try.

I think I achieved both goals even if I had to abandon one of my principles of prose writing. Loose ends abound as my novel ends.

What on earth was I thinking? I should not have done that. I'm too old to write a sequel.

Tom Robson
August 18, 2017

ACKNOWLEDGEMENTS

An aging procrastinator needs help to persevere through the task of writing a novel. As always, Barb, my wife, tolerates my obsessive solitary pursuit and encourages this activation of my aging mind. She also chastises me when I revert to British expressions, as would any caring Canadian. She didn't like the first draft of *Wait and See.* When she reads this version, she may realize that her husband does listen and can improve.

The Evergreen Writers Group of Dartmouth is a most supportive gathering of wannabe writers. There is no apprehension in sharing work in progress with them. Cathy, Phil, and Elizabeth have critiqued this work, which was somewhat sparse and primitive before their input. I owe them.

Cathy MacKenzie, my editor and publisher, should know how much her efforts, in troubled times, were above and beyond. She makes me a better writer.

And those who know you have a book in you, waiting to be released, start it before you reach eighty. You may need time for a sequel.

WAIT AND SEE

A Story of a Romance
and
Its Effects on Those Related

TOM ROBSON

And So It Begins . . .

On a typical late October evening, downtown Halifax, Nova Scotia, is threatened by fog rolling into its harbour from the cold waters of the broad North Atlantic. By morning, only the upper floors of offices, apartments, and condo high rises will see the sunrise and the blue sky. The wooden signal masts on the fortress may be the only sign of Citadel Hill, whose eastern flanks stretch down to the harbour, where the original city blocks were laid out more than 260 years before.

Brad thinks the encroaching fog gives an air of mystery to the buildings and boardwalk it envelopes, but he is also convinced it hides no real danger, disguises no alien threat, and offers insufficient cover for heinous crimes or assaults on the senses. The Friday night revelers will not be surprised by it; neither will it limit their enjoyment of downtown.

As he walks from the restaurant back to his waterfront hotel on this particular Friday evening, the bars, clubs, and taverns are loud and lively, whether already hidden in the fog or illuminated in forlorn hope that the approaching mists will not hide them. The music and, perhaps, the lineups at the door betray their presence. The almost inevitable groups of pub crawlers will locate them, each in turn. Recent arrivals at the city's universities will have become familiar with those offering the best in atmosphere, bargain beer, live music, dancing, illegal substances, and hookup possibilities.

Brad eases into a closed shop doorway while a raucous crew of pub crawlers hasten to the next pint of draught. They are obliviously joyful, a state he, at that moment, envies.

The pubs and clubs generally attract the younger set or those who refuse to give in to maturing years. Yet Brad finds himself being tempted as he walks past various watering holes. The restaurant crowd, if warmed to disinhibition by martinis, wine, and digestif, might opt to relive their youth by dropping into the rowdier spots. Within minutes, they will wonder why. They look for someone to be the first to admit they have outgrown this noise and frenetic dancing. Some even fear meeting their children at a club and being forced to explain their presence at an awkward breakfast the following morning.

Brad is one of these lost minorities of clubbing misfits. He is in town to attend an international conference on alternative forms of energy. He represents his Montreal-based company, which specializes in wind turbines. Though his job requires frequent travel away from his wife and two sons in the Montreal suburb of Kirkland, Quebec, he finds the after-business hours tedious and never-ending. He long ago gave up looking for "adventures abroad" or succumbing to the locals' pressure to join them in an extended evening of drinking while showing him the city's hot spots.

Though he wishes he was back in his five-bedroom home in Montreal, with its pool, hot tub, man cave, and family, Brad detours into Richardson's, a lively bar that offers to delay a too-early night back at his waterfront hotel. Too late, he is reminded that forty-four-year-olds are not the target clientele the management wants to attract. He feels ancient as he gazes at the clothing adorning tattooed, pierced, and supposedly beautiful youth. His hearing is taxed by the music and the impossibility of even shouted conversation, which explains why everyone communes with their mobile devices instead of with their companions.

His instant reaction? One drink and he's gone. Now, where's a seat?

* * *

Kate's presence in that same bar is also unplanned. Her evening out with friends from the hospital where she is a nurse did not have Richardson's on the agenda, but pre-dinner martinis and too much wine with their leisurely meal has fueled their stop-off detour.

Instead of making excuses and finding her car, parked on Brunswick Street where the green grounds of Citadel Hill meets the downtown, she was persuaded to go clubbing. Aware of her mistake, she looks for an opportunity to bail out. Her Clayton Park condo is a fifteen-minute drive away, just off the peninsula, and the hour is not too late to curl up with a good book. But how to escape? Some of her friends, regardless of their attachment status, are on the prowl. They are set to stay for as long as it takes or until common sense prevails over the search for lost years and forbidden adventure.

"On the prowl" comes to mind. She strains to hear their comments and conversation as they revert to the flaunting behaviour most of them left behind fifteen years before. Kate, who accepts that she will never see thirty-nine again, is not even the oldest of the eight. But it seems her behaviour is. She has no desire to look for a man here. Her former, unlamented husband frequented such spots before she naively thought marriage would change his habits. It did, for a while, but his immaturity and chronic infidelity now take them through the divorce courts.

Kate realizes this place isn't for her. Not even after the divorce dust settled would she come here looking for company. Time to leave and go home.

She isn't comfortable breaking into the enjoyment her group either feels or pretends to say her farewells. In a few more minutes, she will sneak off. But, oh God! Her feet are killing her in these new shoes, and it seems as if she and her friends have been standing forever. That's one of the rules of the hook-up game: Stand up so you'll be noticed; sit down after you meet someone.

But Kate isn't in the game, so there must be a seat somewhere.

* * *

Fate brings these two souls together. It is a casual, perhaps fortuitous happenstance. But their meeting has consequences for both of them, and though it doesn't cross their minds in the chaos that is Richardson's, it will affect many to whom Kate and Brad are connected.

Part One

MARITIME INTERLUDE

Sometimes words don't come easily,
especially those long suppressed in the heart.
Sometimes they are launched by impetuosity.

Chapter 1
Mistakes and Meetings

11:00 p.m., Friday, October 23rd
Richardson's Bar, Halifax

All these women jostling around the mirror. If this line-up in the washroom doesn't move, he'll think I've bailed on him. Kate smiled at her thoughts. At least the conversation was interesting. Much more raunchy than when she used to club on a Friday night.

She felt much too old for this. She was past it all. She had even forgotten that bathroom breaks were usually taken with at least one girlfriend, not to mention the interminable wait time for an empty stall.

Finally, a stall became available.

When she eventually leaned over the sink to check herself in the mirror, she wondered why she was renewing her lip gloss and attempting to hide her forty years. What was the word to describe women of her age who hung around clubs and bars? Cougar! She didn't want to be thought of as a "cougar."

As soon as the guy walked her to the car, she was headed home—alone. So what if it was only eleven o'clock. Her days of two-in-the-morning-barhopping with girls were long past.

The weekend was her daughter's time with her father and his bimbo in Bedford. Kate would have the condo to herself. In the morning, she would phone her friends and make up an excuse for abandoning them. She shouldn't have come in the first place, even if it was her weekend off from work. Four full days away from the hospital. The stop at Richardson's would not be a highlight.

Her thoughts reverted to the current predicament. What if the man made a move on her on the way to the car? He didn't seem to be that type, but who knew? He appeared as out of place in the pickup joint as she did.

She adjusted her skirt, collected her jacket, and went to find him.

* * *

Brad hoped the woman hadn't run off instead of going to the ladies' room as she'd said. Maybe she returned to her friends. He had offered to walk her to her car, and perhaps she thought he was making a move on her.

He wasn't sure exactly why he'd entered this crowded, noisy club that played this God-awful music. He'd had a good meal at the restaurant recommended by the secretary in the Halifax office. After dinner, it had been too early to return to his room at the hotel so, on impulse, he'd stepped into the first drinking establishment he passed—Richardson's. As soon as he stepped in, forcing his way toward the bar, he knew he'd made a mistake. This was not a crowd in which he felt comfortable. Any remote ideas he had about meeting someone—and-who-knew-what—quickly disappeared.

But since he was there, he'd look anyway. No harm in that. And he'd never gone farther than looking. Given the current state of his marriage, maybe he should. There had been opportunities.

His wife, Jill, back in Kirkland, would take every advantage of his weekend absence to spend time with Aaron, the man she had said she loved. Brad hoped Jill was discrete. Their two boys were at ages they might suspect their mother played around if she wasn't careful. Maybe not James, but Harry was old enough to wonder. Perhaps she was taking the opportunity to tell their teenage sons about Aaron. She had been unpredictable recently; he wouldn't put anything past her. And she didn't feel obliged to share information with Brad, even when it concerned their sons.

As soon as he entered Richardson's, he'd spotted a pair of empty chairs in a secluded corner. Like a clubbing amateur, he sat, removing himself from the circulating throng of opportunists. He would keep his one-drink-and-gone promise.

He gazed around at the crowd of young people trying too hard to present an image meant to impress. Some were a sight to behold. How many of the girls' parents knew their daughters were dressed so skimpily and provocatively and flaunting it in a casual hook-up bar like this? He supposed it was chauvinistic to feel relief that he had sons and not daughters, so he quickly dismissed that idea, defending it with a realization that times had changed since he'd been on the dating scene more than twenty years previously. Now the uninhibited placed everything out for inspection.

While he'd been watching the scene, a demure, fashionably dressed woman detached herself from a similar group clustered by the bar. As she pushed her way through the crowd between his quiet nook and her friends, he realized she was no mutton-dressed-as-lamb regular. She was eye-catching, older than the target clientele, out of place, and—she was headed his way. Would she talk to him? What was happening? Suddenly, he had felt nervous and sweaty.

"Is this chair taken?" She'd leaned over. "If not, my feet and I would love to keep you company."

He tried not to gaze at the brief display of cleavage. "Take the weight off," he responded, looking down at stiletto heels sinking into the fading carpet. "New shoes?"

"Too new, too dressy, and not made for these hilly Halifax streets." She sat and placed her drink on the small table between them. "I even have to take them off to drive. What we women do for fashion." She laughed.

The small talk had continued. Brad relaxed. He had to lean in close to make himself heard and wondered if one purpose of the high volume, ear-splitting music was intended to promote such proximity. He explained how he'd come to be in Richardson's, letting her know he was in unaccustomed and uncomfortable territory, yet also pleased she sat with him.

The lights, other than those flashing on the dance floor, were dim. Unobtrusively, he took a closer look at his new companion, guessing her age to be close to his—no, a few years younger; not yet forty.

She was tall and shapely, with short dark hair and eyes that looked blue behind the fashionable glasses. The gloss made her full lips a little too scarlet for his taste, but what did he know. Her skirt had ridden up when she sat, displaying long, legging-clad legs. He hoped when she stood that she wasn't taller than he was. She was certainly slimmer. What the hell? Who cared if she was taller? He wasn't in the greatest shape, and most certainly he wasn't in the hookup game. He figured she wasn't either. Relax, he'd told himself. Enjoy the company.

She said her nursing friends from work had convinced her to join the girls' night out, which she'd assumed would be drinks, dinner, and then home. But it promised to be a long night if she kept pace with her friends. As Brad leaned in even closer to discover more about this intriguing woman, she shared discomfort being in the bar, where she was older than most of the female patrons. She confessed she'd love to sneak away early and added that her car was parked nearby.

Had he received a message—the wrong message? Was he being subtly propositioned? He was attracted to this personable lady, who shared more of herself with every passing minute, and the more she did, the more attracted he'd become.

But the possible implication of her last statements clearly embarrassed her. She was flustered, which only made her more attractive when she blushingly tried to correct the impression she wanted to escape with him.

She rambled, and though he didn't know why, she said she was in the process of a divorce and her sixteen-year-old daughter, Jenny, was staying with her ex through the weekend. The more she struggled to explain, the more uncomfortable she became. Every hint that implied she was available was countered by a message that she wasn't.

Brad had wanted to intervene, sensing her discomfort and needing to get her away from relationship issues. Thankfully, their seats were hemmed in by the growing crowd. He had the impression she would have walked away from her embarrassment if she'd been able.

He tried to give what he hoped was reassurance. "You're like me in this place. A fish out of water." And then he apologized for the unflattering image. He confessed he was married but neglected to add the marriage was in the process of disintegration. That deliberate omission was intended to let the woman know that, even if she was casting a hook, he was trying to avoid swallowing it. "But," he added, "I'm enjoying your company, so can I do you two favours before I go back to the hotel?"

"That depends on what they're going to cost me. And why are you in a hotel?" She flashed a smile, indicating relief that he had stopped her embarrassing ramblings.

"Favours are free. I'm in town until Sunday for the alternative energy conference. I live in Montreal—well, the West Island. Kirkland." He smiled back, hoping his tightening facial muscles hadn't turned his smile into a smirk. "Can I buy you a drink so we can talk a little longer? Then I'll walk you to your car if you still want to escape early, like me."

As an afterthought, he added, "No strings!"

She'd accepted both offers. Their conversation became more general, less personal and, thankfully, relaxed. They busied themselves by speculating on the appearances and pretenses on display, amused at their increasingly ridiculous suggestions as to the subjects of the impossible-to-hear conversations and texts between certain couples. When speculations turned suggestive, they became more comfortable with each another, but to escape the risqué content, they had resorted to the tried and true topic shared with strangers—their children.

The shouting and laughter from the ladies' room transported Brad back to the present. Where was she? He had paid the bill and waited a few feet from the washroom door.

He hadn't realized he'd been so nervous until she emerged. He let out a breath, not only pleased he was taller, even if only a half inch or so, but that she had reappeared. He grasped her arm, helping her through the crowds congregated inside and outside the club doorway. The cool fall evening was refreshing after the stuffiness of the bar.

The walk to the car was uphill, away from his hotel. Her fashionable pumps dangled from their straps, gripped by the hand he might have been tempted to hold had it been empty. Offering to carry her, even as a joke, might have been open to misinterpretation as well as laughter. He mentioned that to her, and she did laugh.

At the car, she asked where he was staying and offered to drive him since it was on her way. But the thought of separating from this easy-to-know lady and the prospect of returning to an impersonal hotel room depressed him.

After he fastened his seatbelt, she turned and said, "I don't think I've told you, but my name is Kate. And thanks for rescuing me from what was becoming a painfully long and late night."

"Glad to have met you, Kate. I'm Brad. And you turned a mistake I made into a pleasant experience. I'm glad I met you. Really glad."

She drove to the Historic Properties Hotel entrance. An awkward silence was disrupted by a tap on the window. Kate wound it down, and the car jockey asked, "Ma'am, what's your room number, please. Will you need the car before morning?"

She turned to Brad. When he opened his mouth to reply, she interjected, loudly and clearly, "No, we won't be going anywhere until after breakfast. Brad, what was our room number again?"

Passing the keys to the car jockey, she collected her shoes, got out of the car, and joined the astounded Brad on the hotel steps. He stuttered as he said 8023 to the grinning car jockey.

They walked into the lobby. Brad carried her shoes in one clammy hand. His other grasped Kate's.

* * *

Why is my heart pounding? Kate didn't know Brad, but the spontaneous and untypical moves she'd made at the hotel entrance seemed so right. He must be wondering what was going on. And then there was his wife.

No! Don't go there!

As soon as they reached the room, she would clarify the situation. Wouldn't she?

She had acted impetuously when they pulled into the hotel forecourt. While enjoying the drink conversation with Brad, she had felt comfortable with him. There was no threat in his presence. He wasn't putting on an act or even making a phony, passive approach. He seemed to be himself, and it was a self that became increasingly appealing.

She had sensed he wouldn't issue an invitation to his hotel room. A part of her had been suppressed for too long, and she didn't want the evening to end. Would it continue in his room?

Perhaps the raunchy conversations in Richardson's washroom had prompted the slip in her inhibitions. Her unexpected response to the car jockey's inquiry would give her the opportunity to gain more time with Brad—alone. She didn't know how they'd spend that time, but she wasn't closing her mind to any possibilities with this attractive man.

Chapter 2
Plans and Conditions

Close to midnight, Friday, October 23rd
Historic Properties Hotel, Halifax

As he rescued the plastic from his wallet, Brad silently prayed the key card would work. The last thing he wanted was to return to reception with Kate. He doubted whether he could string two words of explanation together if that happened.

The green light flashed above the door handle. Brad opened it and stepped back to usher Kate into the room.

What now? he wondered, almost grateful his bladder reacted and he could mutter an excuse to shut himself in the bathroom. That problem was much easier to relieve than his uncertainty about how to proceed once on the other side of the door, back in the bedroom.

* * *

When Kate turned to face Brad with questions he might not like and which could kill the mood, tenuous as it was, he mumbled and turned into the bathroom. This gave her time to think. Equally important was how she could ask about his wife. The position she'd put herself in had the potential for so many disastrous embarrassments. How could she avoid them and prolong the enjoyment she experienced since meeting this man, who was easy to converse with and undemanding? Maybe she should throw herself at him and see what happened.

She scanned the obviously expensive room, her gaze ignoring the bed that offered possibilities to which she was not yet totally committed. For a man's hotel room, it was remarkably tidy. His laptop and a neat pile of files and papers were on a table, flanked by empty chairs.

When the toilet flushed, she sank into the far chair, crossed her legs, and watched Brad exit the bathroom and walk past the bed to the other chair. She hadn't been mistaken. In the bright light, she confirmed her initial impression that he was good looking. He was a little taller than she was—

or would be when she wasn't wearing the ridiculous heels. The jacket of the suit he'd been wearing was too expensive to be casually thrown on the bed with the tie he'd also discarded. His short brown hair was fashionably styled, with a hint of grey at the temples. Late-night stubble showed on his tanned face, which featured a strong chin and sensuous lips. His hypnotic eyes would be even more captivating in a relaxed situation.

Her thoughts, as she checked him out, were becoming distinctly erotic, and she wondered what she really wanted.

The too-long silence was interrupted when she said, "I need to know . . ." at the same time Brad said, "I don't know. . ."

The second embarrassing silence ended when he invited her to speak first.

She was sure she could convert her jumbled thoughts into questions that wouldn't spoil the precariously balanced moment, but what came from her mouth was all wrong. "Back in Richardson's, you said you had a wife. So, what are we doing here?"

He remained seated, open-mouthed, and she sensed he was as uncertain in his answer as she had been with her question. He probably had explanations ready, but they would have vanished behind nerves, wondering how much to reveal.

"Oh, that's not what I meant to say. I invited myself up here. But . . ." How could she phrase her words into a non-threatening question? "If I'm going to stay, I need to know about your wife—and you. I don't do one-night stands."

Brad's silence was disconcerting, so she pushed. "Talk to me, Brad. Do I stay or leave? What's going on right now? After the number I pulled at the hotel entrance, you'd think I'd know what I'm doing, but I don't. That was impulsive and way out of character. Now I'm questioning myself as well as you. Talk to me. Please!"

He slumped, elbows on knees, looking at his feet. There was another threatening silence until he straightened, turned to look her in the eye, and leaned on the round table separating them. His words were measured. "If you want to leave after I've finished, I'll be sorry. But I'll understand."

She was touched by the sadness in his blue eyes. She placed a hand on his tightly clenched fist and felt him relax when he continued.

"This is the truth even though it will sound like a pack of lies designed to get you off that chair and into that bed."

Kate squeezed his hand in reassurance. "I'm listening."

"If you were to ask me where my wife is now, I'd say she is probably in bed at her lover's apartment in Pointe Claire. She will be reluctant to leave but has to make the fifteen-minute drive home to our sons soon. Before she does, she and Aaron will have arranged when and where they can meet tomorrow and Sunday, before I get back. On Sunday evening, Jill and I will again pretend we are a loving couple in a happy family, but we're not."

She uttered a strangled, "Oh no."

He ignored it. "When I got back from a conference in Frankfurt in May, Jill told me she was in love with Aaron, had been seeing him regularly, and that she would be leaving me to be with him when the time was right."

"I don't understand. Why keep you dangling like that? She sounds like a real—" All this information was difficult to process even without the underlying question, *Am I hearing the truth?*

She was astounded her question brought forth so much personal information. This man was not your run-of-the-mill seducer. He either had a very polished line or was being more open and honest than he needed to be on a casual date.

"No, she can be a cow, but she is waiting until she thinks James, our thirteen-year-old, can deal with his parents splitting up. He's a real mommy's boy." He paused and smiled. "I'm being too harsh. He's a good kid, but very naive. I suspect Harry—he's seventeen—knows what's going on but is pretending not to. In the meantime, Jill sees Aaron as often as she can, and I turn a blind eye to it."

Kate sensed he wished he hadn't revealed so much but felt compelled to continue. "Of course, I know we can't keep on this way. Sometime we have to resolve this situation and explain it to the boys. Harry is in CEGEP—junior college—and, as I think I told you before, should be heading down here to Dalhousie in September. And now I'm beginning to ramble."

"No, you're not." She hesitated while forming her next questions. "How can you live like that, the two of you? You can't keep on like that. How about you? Have you got a sweet young secretary tucked away somewhere in Montreal?" She wanted to hear that this lovely man, with the cow of a wife, was not a serial philanderer seeking revenge on women at every opportunity. If he was, she had gotten herself into an impossible situation.

"Short version is," Brad continued, "my wife loves someone else and is determined to leave me at some point. We have separate beds, and I don't have a sweet young thing or an understanding older woman on the side. Nobody, not even our parents, has a clue that our marriage is a sham. Except Jill has probably shared tales of her adventures with her best friend, Chrissie, who hates me. She probably thinks I drove Jill into Aaron's bed and that I'm a heartless, useless husband. But I'm not."

She resisted the impulse to interrupt. It amazed her how much he was unloading. He continued quietly with what she perceived as sincerity. "I'd love it if you stayed with me a little longer. It's so good to talk to a woman without arguing or having to measure words and keep secrets or pretend.

And honestly, I'm not pretending with you. You're the first person I've really talked to about Jill and me."

Kate viewed this hurting man. She didn't have much experience dealing with men who spewed lies to get women into their beds, but her instincts told her that Brad was telling the truth. Not that the truth was too easy to deal with either.

She needed time to think, so she stood and stepped toward the bathroom. "My turn." Passing him, she leaned over to kiss the spot where his short hair touched his brow. He reached for her, but she wriggled away.

In the bathroom, she was about to pull up her leggings when she stopped, took them off, and stuck them in her purse. She was glad she had shaved her legs before heading out for the evening. Her skirt was really too short to wear without the leggings, but she had made a decision. She checked herself in the mirror, pulling the skirt down as far as it would go, and reminded herself not to bend over. Then she thought again. *Hell! Why not? I can tell him, or I can show him that I'm staying. Whatever happens, happens!*

She flushed, walked purposefully back into the bedroom, and as ladylike as possible, she lay on her side on the bed, revealing her long, slim legs up to the flimsiest underwear she owned. Maybe she'd worn Victoria's Secret as a subconscious wish to get into a compromising situation but quickly thrust that notion to the back of her mind.

She stared at Brad. When he neither said anything nor moved, not even a flinch, she offered words of encouragement. "This is what I'm thinking, Brad. You're an honest man, which is a rare breed in this day and age. I'd love to talk some more. I don't know what else you have to share, but I know you must have questions about my divorce." She held out her hand. "Please come over here."

He had already removed his shoes, and he came to her, his arm reaching round her. Their faces were inches apart on the pillow.

"Thank you, Kate! I never . . ." He seemed afraid of another silence.

She quieted him with a gentle finger on his lips. "Brad whatever-your-last-name-is, you're a lovely man, but you need to hear me before you say anything else. My intention is to make love to you. I hope this won't just be a slam-bam-thank-you-ma'am sex. If we do make love, I hope to see you tomorrow and Sunday before you go back to Montreal. We have two days to discover if that's all there is, and we can both say thank you and goodbye."

* * *

Brad had difficulty believing what he was hearing. A pick-up in a bar! It wasn't supposed to be like this. Nor the promise of sex. Forget that word. He hoped he could make love the way she expected and not make a hash of it. You weren't supposed to meet someone this way and finish up in your hotel room, with the woman looking for a relationship that wasn't just sex and a disappearance into the night.

He broke the silence. "Kate whatever-*your*-surname-is, I love the way you think, and I agree to your conditions and want to add one of my own."

"Uh, uh. My name is Kathryn Hull. My maiden name. I'm using Newman until my divorce comes through. Now, give it to me! Your condition, I mean." She smiled.

He laughed at her careless use of an expression. "I could stay in town until Monday morning. That way we can have three evenings together, but I have to work Saturday until four and Sunday until midday. I can change my flight if—" He did a quick switch without killing his proposal. "Did you have plans for Sunday?"

She hesitated, and he wondered if she'd decline.

"None, except my daughter comes home midafternoon."

"If I'm not on my Sunday afternoon flight, maybe I can meet her. You can introduce me as Brad Anderson. And that's my real name." He chuckled.

Was he moving too far and too fast? It seemed so right. How could any of this be wrong?

His belief was answered and emphasized when Kate pulled his head toward her so their lips met in what became a kiss that led to much more.

Chapter 3
Addictions and Deceptions

1:00 a.m., Saturday, October 24th
Lakeside Condominiums, Pointe Claire, PQ

Aaron wondered how Jill could be so lithe and limber at her age. Her leg extended across his thigh, and her fingers teased his nipple. The woman couldn't get enough. How old was she? She had to be forty-five, way past the thirty-eight she owned up to.

His mind often wandered after sex. No wonder women felt shut out when it was over. That post-prandial ennui was accompanied, in his case, by the post-sex cigarette. Which was better? That smoke or the first one in the morning?

He returned to Jill, at least his wandering mind did. Any minute she'd want to talk. Either that, or go again. Did she think he was an inexhaustible eighteen-year-old? But he went pretty good for someone twice that age.

Instead, she disentangled herself from the scarlet silk sheets she'd bought him for his birthday and disappeared into the washroom.

He was mystified by Jill's husband's indifference. She had told him that Brad knew what was going on. Brad's travelling gave Aaron and Jill ample opportunity to meet, but Brad could have objected and demanded that his wife stop straying. Aaron's thoughts wandered to Jill's boys. He was sure the oldest must clue in that his mom was playing away from home.

Maybe it was time to bring this situation to a close before something exploded. Where was the relationship going, anyway? Maybe Jill was serious, but he didn't want to contemplate the implications of that. Perhaps it was time to let her go, even help her on her way.

His mind wandered back to his obsession. *The sex is so good. She's a fucking contortionist. So what if she's older than me? Maybe she's only a couple of years older.*

His meanderings were interrupted when Jill emerged from the bathroom, blatantly naked, and sorted her underwear from the jumbled pile of clothing on the floor. "I guess I have to get home to the boys."

She was as sexy putting her clothes back on as she was when removing them. Dressed or undressed, the lady had both class and an abundance of sex appeal. Her petite body was incredibly shaped, topped with short blonde hair that always seemed casually tousled but never disheveled. Aaron considered her absence of inhibition her best quality.

"You're not listening again! Men are all the same after they're satisfied. Don't want to hear anything or say anything." Jill's voice disturbed his phantasy reverie.

"I wish you could stay all night," he lied.

"Soon." She covered her messy hair with a fluffy hat. "I'll see you about seven tomorrow. Where can we go for dinner? How about going into town? One of those restaurants on the Plateau?"

"Sounds good." He gave the expected response and faked enthusiasm. The thought they were becoming like a married couple crossed his mind. He reminded himself that he'd been there, done that; he didn't want to do it again—with Jill or anyone.

She retrieved her purse from the table and leaned in to kiss him. Her free hand reached toward his naked body. "It was great. Maybe I just love you for the sex and this . . . this thing. But I don't think so."

She pecked him again on the lips before breaking apart. She swung her sexy butt provocatively while she strode to the door.

She was getting too serious. She's got to go, Aaron thought, too tired to think how he could arrange it and whether he could persuade her to be available only for sex, now and again.

* * *

Jill drove the slow route along Lakeshore Boulevard to St. Charles and across to Kirkland. Traffic was quiet, and she had time to ponder. Again she decided she couldn't continue with her marriage. Brad knew how she felt about Aaron. Harry, at nearly eighteen, would understand. Then she and Brad could sort out living arrangements. James might be a problem, but . . .

That was the fragile thread that kept her and Brad together. And it was ridiculous. Her happiness unattainable because James, her thirteen-year-old, was super-sensitive? When Brad returned, they would need another discussion. She must be with Aaron or she would lose him to one of the bimbos he used to date. Who knows, maybe he dated them when Brad was home and she couldn't get together with Aaron as frequently as she liked.

She ought to discuss their future with Aaron. He must know how much she loved him. Did he think she was just a raunchy female who wasn't getting enough at home? They were beginning to go places together, doing things other than athletic and satisfying lovemaking. She could handle living in his apartment though there wasn't room for the boys. But Aaron would move. He had mentioned his lease was up in December and was thinking of moving. Should she continue to keep her age secret or confess to her forty-five years? No, Aaron wasn't ready for that. Not yet.

As she pulled into her garage, she knew she had to talk to the two men in her life. And soon. This couldn't go on.

* * *

Just as Aaron drifted into sleep, his phone rang. *What does she want now?* he thought, checking the number.

But it wasn't Jill.

"Where are you, baby? I thought you were going to be here tonight. I miss you, baby."

The French accent and slurred speech made identification by voice difficult. He scanned the call display again but didn't recognise the name. He gambled that he knew who it was.

"Sophia. Ma petite! I would have loved to meet you there, but I had to take clients out to dinner, and by the time we finished talking business it was too late to find you. I miss you, sweetie. Where are you now?"

Bingo! He'd guessed right. Earlier in the week, while trawling in a bar on the Plateau, he'd met a gorgeous girl of Italian extraction, a student at Universite de Montreal. He'd made the mistake of using the French "Sophie," but she corrected him, saying her father insisted on the Italian name of her grandmother.

They had talked and flirted for hours, but even with all the drinks he'd bought her, she played hard to get after he drove her back to her apartment. Though the Porsche impressed her, all he got was Sophia's promise that next time she'd invite him up. That, together with the enthusiasm of the goodbye kiss, implied much.

Aaron suddenly remembered that she had his number and they had half arranged to meet earlier.

"But you promised!" the drunken voice on the phone said. "You don't want me, do you?"

"It's too late tonight," he said, thinking fast while he poured excuses. Then he remembered Jill's husband would be back on Sunday. "Remind me where you live, and I'll pick you up at six on Sunday, and we can go for a drive and dinner. How's that?"

Aaron scrambled for a pen when Sophia gabbled, "5729 rue de Bienville, apartment 224. I'm not home yet. But if you promise to go there now, I'll get a taxi and be waiting for you. Please, Aaron?"

Five minutes later, wondering how a student could afford an apartment in that upscale area, he pulled on his jeans and headed for the Plateau. He'd promised Sophia he'd be there by 2:00 a.m. He hoped she'd make it home and wouldn't fall asleep before he got there. He also hoped he could make a quick recovery. The promise of sex with that gorgeous twenty-year-old had been held out to him, which did wonders for the libido.

Chapter 4
Suspicion and Confirmation

2:00 a.m., Saturday, October 24th
Treetops Terrace, Kirkland, PQ

Harry saw the lights when the car turned into the driveway and glanced at his phone. Close to two in the morning. Hard as he tried to stay awake, he guessed he'd fallen asleep. The remote was beside him in the recliner. He exited the den and was waiting for his mother when she entered from the garage.

He had prepared himself for more lies from his mother. What would be her excuse this time? Rather than let her initiate the story she would have already invented for the cover-up, Harry decided to take the offensive. He'd swallowed too many lies, and his unquestioning acceptance encouraged her attempts to fool his father and his brother.

But no more. Not him!

His speech was ready.

* * *

Jill hesitated after she closed the car door. Either someone was awake or they'd left the TV on in the den. She hoped it wasn't Harry. She ran through the story in her mind one more time, hoping it wouldn't be needed until morning.

God, she was tired. A full day's work in the office and showing those new condos to that couple from Cornwall, who had no intention of buying, had made her late for everything. Late feeding the boys. Late leaving the house. Late getting to Aaron's. And now late getting home though she couldn't blame the Cornwall couple for that.

She steeled herself when she entered the house. There was Harry. She looked past him, but James must be in bed asleep. Before she had a chance to say anything, Harry thrust his chin forward and accused her. She figured he had convinced himself that his mother was living a lie that needed correcting, for it quickly became apparent that he knew about Aaron, although maybe not his name or other details.

Though she realized it was futile, she tried to stall the inevitable disagreement. "Do we have to talk about this now, Harry? Can it wait till morning? It's late, and we're both too tired to talk sense. Off you go to bed. I'll tidy up."

The casual, matter-of-fact tone didn't deter her son, and he sounded more annoyed.

"Two o'clock, Mom. Where have you been this time? And I know you've been seeing someone when Dad's away. I'm not a kid any more. And I'm not stupid."

She listened to his obviously rehearsed speech, amazed at the accuracy of his allegations. He accused her of seeing "some guy called Aaron Drapkin," who kept calling her cellphone and the home phone.

"You could only be doing one thing on those nights you were out 'til all hours whenever Dad was away. And don't say you were with Aunt Chrissie. She phoned one night when you were supposed to be with her. She's a worse liar than you. And don't tell me any more lies. I'm old enough to deserve the truth."

Jill almost gave him the Jack Nicholson line from one of his movies: "You can't handle the truth!" But the time for lies and deceit had long passed, and her son deserved a version of the truth, whether he could handle it or not.

"Keep your voice down, Harry. The last thing we want to do is wake James. And what were you doing? Sneaking into my cell?"

"That's not the point. The point is where have you been until two in the morning?"

Her son had her boxed into a corner. Lies weren't going to work. Wasn't it children who gave half-truths as alibis when returning home late? The role reversal amused her for a second until she remembered the current crisis. "Okay, let's go sit in the den, and I'll try to explain."

Harry turned and shuffled to the den. He turned off the television, slumped into the armchair, and stretched his feet over the footstool. He mumbled that she never told the truth.

Where had time gone? A short while ago, he'd been a confused and rebellious, but sweet, teenager. She marveled that not only was he maturing to physically resemble his father, his attitudes and conversation habits were similar, too. There wasn't much spontaneity with either of them. Everything was thought through before an utterance. Actions were planned and consequences evaluated, before as well as after. She guessed that Harry had more questions and accusations. Maybe even evidence, real and inferred. Just as his father would.

She shoved the footstool, forcing Harry to sit straighter. He glared at her as if ready with more accusations and evidence should she lie.

She breathed deeply and jumped in before he could start. "I'm sorry about this, Harry. But this is what's going on."

Words tumbled from her mouth, and her son knew better than to interrupt. She began at the summer before last when she found herself unhappy, in an emotional rut, and restless. She no longer loved his dad and didn't know whether he loved her. By the time winter was over, she had found it almost impossible to lead a normal life, which is why she spent so much time at exercise classes and yoga. She was in two book clubs with Aunt Chrissie. Anything to get out of the routine of work and looking after—

She switched gears quickly. "When I was out for dinner one night last spring, with Chrissie and a couple of girls from work, I was introduced to Aaron Drapkin, who was a friend of Aunt Chrissie. She gave him my cell number when he asked her for it. She shouldn't have done that, but she did.

"He called and invited me out while your dad was away somewhere or other. I should have said no, but I didn't. Long story short—we fell in love, and I've been seeing him ever since, as often as I could."

Before Harry spouted more condemnations, she added, "I told your father what had happened, back at the start of summer. It wasn't fair to keep going behind his back. Even if I don't love him anymore, he's still a nice man and a good father." She smiled.

Harry piped up, "You got that right!"

She ignored him. "We've kept pretending everything is normal because of you and James. Maybe you were old enough to understand, but we dreaded what it would do to James. I was waiting until I thought he could deal with the change, and then we could work out what to do. Maybe that was just an excuse to avoid confrontations like this, but your dad and I can't stay together this way. I have Aaron now, and when it's right, we're going to move in together. I love Aaron, Harry. You must meet him soon. He drives a Porsche and skis at Bromont all winter."

"So what."

Jill knew when it was time to keep quiet. She waited for the torrent of questions from her son, who seemed to struggle to sort and articulate them. Each time he tried to speak, he gave up.

She tried to help. "That's my short version of events. Hurtful and selfish though it may be, it's the truth as I see it. When your father gets back tomorrow, he'll give you his side, and we can move on from there. But please don't say anything to James until we decide when and what he can be told." She waited for a response before she asked, "Do you have any questions that won't keep until we've both had some sleep?"

Harry gazed back at her, with a hurtful and confused expression, and seemed unable to form his words.

Jill was relieved. "No? Then we should both head upstairs though I doubt I can sleep after this, exhausted as I am." She wanted to cry and leap over to hug him and offer words and idle promises of consolation.

"I don't know how you can do this to us. I think it's selfish. And I wish I didn't love you cos right now, I hate you! And yes, I have questions. But I'll ask Dad before I ask you. He doesn't lie! How can you give up all this? How can you split us apart like this?"

She had no reply except tears that flooded as soon as her angry son leaped from the chair and stormed up the stairs.

* * *

Not bothering to undress, Harry flung himself on the bed, his mind a jumble of confused facts, emotions, and half-formed questions. If he was this screwed up, what would it do to James?

What to do? The easy answer was nothing because it was too late to do anything until morning. He wished his father was home. But if he had been, then his mother would not have been out the previous night, and her supposedly true story would not have been shared—if what his mother had told him was the truth. He had to talk to his father when he returned, hopefully before his mom did. She probably knew the hotel number and might be phoning him now or waking him on his mobile.

Harry would try his father before his meetings in Halifax, and when he came home, they could both knock sense into his mother.

What the hell was going to happen because—

"Shit! Shit! Shit!" He yelled and hoped his mother hadn't heard. Not that he cared.

Sure enough, two minutes later, she tapped on the door and peered in. The back light revealed enough of her features for Harry to tell she'd been crying. Serves her right, he thought.

"I'm sorry," she pleaded. "I really am."

"Go away before I tell you to fuck off," he said.

Chapter 5
Complaints and Confessions

8:00 a.m., Saturday, October 24th
Phone from Highway Condominiums, Bedford, to Clayton Park, Halifax

As much as Jenny tried, sleep was beyond her despite being awake half the night. She was in the smaller of the two bedrooms in the condominium that her father rented. The bedroom next door was occupied by her dad and Suzie, his girlfriend. It wasn't the first no-sleep night Jenny had experienced on weekends with her father.

She wanted to phone her mom to ask if she could sleep at home on Saturday night, but her mother would say that wouldn't be fair to her father. Did her mother even know that her ex-husband—Jenny's father—spent more time with and paid more attention to sexy Suzie than he did his daughter on the weekends he had visitation?

Jenny studied herself in the mirror, wondering whether to put up her thick, brown hair. Her mother didn't like the highlights, probably because Suzie had suggested it and it hadn't been mom-approved. Suzie had paid for the streaks though Jenny was certain the money had been her father's.

She hoped her dad and Suzie remembered the new jeans they'd promised her. The ones she was wearing were a little tight, suitable only for school and not for going out, even to the mall. She wondered again about asking her mother if she could get a part-time job to pay for clothes and stuff, but her mom would say a job would distract her from school. Silly, really, because she could walk through most classes except for calculus, but her mother demanded high marks and pushed her toward nursing. Jenny wasn't sure that was the career path she wanted to follow.

She sometimes gave her mother a hard time. Kate tried hard not to be a control freak, and she wasn't. What would her mother do when she discovered her daughter was dating the Grade 12 boy who introduced himself as, "I'm Ronnie with the rotten reputation"?

But Ronnie was funny and cool. And hot! Her mom might see those qualities—though not the "hot" part. His reputation was based on lies told by other girls and his own bravado.

Jenny returned to the present. Time she checked in with her mom. Nothing would happen until her father and Suzie woke up. She picked up her cell and punched in the numbers.

Why wasn't her mother answering? She was always awake by this time, and Jenny needed to talk before her father and Suzie woke, if they ever did. Their shenanigans had gone on most of the night. The walls of the condo were thin, and Suzie was a noisy cow. Jenny didn't want to think about what had been playing on the bedroom TV or the laptop while her dad and that—well, the boys at school would have a name for Suzie.

She shuddered imagining what her dad and his girlfriend had been up to. She couldn't stand another night here. Where was her mom?

She tried calling her mother's mobile again.

* * *

"Is that your mobile?" An unfamiliar voice cut through Kate's half-asleep dreamscape. Her eyes sprung open, and she came back to a reality that had changed overnight. Brad held out her large purse, where from its depths her mobile buzzed. She fished it out and saw Jenny's name and number.

"It's my daughter. I have to take this. Sorry!"

Water dripped from Brad's chest and into the towel he had wrapped around him.

"That's all right," he said. He disappeared into the bathroom, shutting the door behind him.

Kate immediately started apologizing to her daughter. This was like a TV show or a movie, she thought, until her distraught daughter cut off her musings.

"Where were you? You always answer right away. I need to talk. I need to come home. I hate it here. I—"

"Stop. Count to five. Why do you need to come home?"

As soon as she heard Jenny's complaints, she became aware of the implications of this turn of events. She wished this wasn't happening. Not today. Couldn't all this wait until Sunday? It was Mike's turn to look after Jenny. Just like him to find a way to screw up things for her.

After seconds of silence, Jenny spoke again. "It's gross!" Without embarrassment, she described the bedroom antics of her beloved father and the "tart"—Jenny's word—that he lived with. "I can hear every sound, Mom. I don't want to listen to all that again. Please, come get me."

It was Kate's turn to count to five. She hadn't realized her innocent (she hoped) daughter was so sexually aware. She thought fast. *I sure as hell can't tell Jenny where I am and what happened last night. It's "comfort, calm, and stall time." But no lies.*

“I hear you, sweetie. First, let’s remember that it’s Dad’s weekend with you and he loves you. I’ll try to talk to him this afternoon. Not sure what I’ll say, but I’ll think of something.”

Most certainly, she would tell her soon-to-be ex-husband to cool his noisy sexual activity with Bimbo Suzie because their daughter was being turned off. That would be an interesting phone conversation. But wouldn’t it be hypocritical after her night with Brad?

“Sometimes I can’t stand Suzie. She acts like she’s my sister, my younger sister. Can you imagine your younger sister having sex with your father! It’s more than gross.”

Kate cut off her daughter’s tirade with a guffaw of genuine laughter. “But aren’t you and Suzie going shopping this afternoon, Jen?”

“If they ever get out of bed!”

“And isn’t the deal that Dad is funding those jeans you want? And a top to go with them?” Kate’s distract and stall tactic seemed to be working because her daughter was listening instead of complaining. “I can meet you for lunch in Bedford and drop you off at two wherever you’re going shopping. Will that work? Where would you like to eat?”

“Cha Baa Thai?” Jenny was quick to suggest.

“Good idea,” Kate agreed. “Let’s meet there at twelve.”

“You will talk to Dad today, won’t you, Mom? Either that or come and take me home.”

As much as I love you, that’s not going to happen, Kate thought. “Let’s see what happens when I talk to your father.”

“Text me after you’ve talked to him.”

“I’ll do that. See you at twelve.” Kate breathed a sigh of relief that she’d sidetracked her daughter. Ever since Kate had kicked out Jenny’s father, she had kept very little from her daughter. Now she had a secret she wasn’t sure she could share—yet. Saying nothing to her about the recent events in her own life might be best, but before she could decide whether and how much to tell Jenny, she and Brad had a few getting-to-know-you items to discuss over breakfast.

Brad peered from the bathroom, grinning. “I can’t wait to meet this daughter of yours.”

After he vacated the bathroom, she sprang from bed. Naked, she walked provocatively to the shower.

* * *

Jenny ended the phone call, realizing her mother had done it again by using Dad’s money to bribe her with a pair of jeans. Jenny couldn’t deny Suzie was fun to shop with. She bought her makeup and facials. Yes, the day would be good, but she wanted to sleep in her own bed in Clayton Park that night. She'd have to work on her mom at lunch.

She heard movement in the other bedroom that sounded like one of them was up. Then the ensuite toilet flushed.

A few minutes later, Suzie shouted, "Coffee's made!"

Her dad's voice replied, "Sounds good! Be right out."

When Jenny entered the kitchen, Suzie asked, "Ready to shop?"

"You got that right," Jenny said, wondering how young Suzie was. Too young for her father, she decided. She had told her mother that Suzie acted too much like a younger sister, but she even dressed like one.

Chapter 6
Breakfast and Break-up

9:00 a.m., Saturday, October 24th
Historic Properties Hotel, Halifax

***I** could get used to this*, Kate thought, while Brad brought the room service breakfast to the table. She was checking her mobile for texts. There was only one new one, from one of the women she'd started out with the previous evening, asking how she was, whether she got home safely, and what happened.

Kate texted back: "Good! Yes! Later! LOL."

Brad poured coffee. As she sipped, she thought how she'd lucked out. So considerate. She remembered the slow and patient way he had made love until her nervous inhibitions disintegrated and her body's response took over. Passion consumed her during those timeless moments. And then, instead of rolling over, believing both were satisfied, he held her close, and his caresses and exploration brought another seemingly never-ending surrender to each other. Even the sleep that followed while they spooned was part of the lovemaking.

Yes, she had lucked out and wanted to shout it to the world. But how could she tell anyone that after months of abstinence, she'd experienced the most incredible sex.

Her memories corrected themselves. She had said she was going to make love to him, but instead he made love to her.

She shook herself from her reverie. Brad, the lover she'd met less than twelve hours previously, was speaking.

* * *

Brad felt the time was right to tell Kate the decision he'd made early that morning. Without preamble, he ploughed ahead. "Before I leave for my conference, I need to tell you something." He pushed away the plate containing sparse remains of scrambled egg, toast, and bacon.

There was no response from Kate.

"While I was lying there this morning, watching you sleep and feeling so contented, I came to a decision. I think I've waited—I mean, we've waited long enough. My marriage is a farce. When I get home on Monday, I'm going to tell Jill that it's time we sorted out our lives and separated. The boys will just have to accept what was going to happen sooner or later anyway."

Kate had a stunned look on her face.

"Well?" he prompted.

"I . . . I hope this isn't just because of last night. Because you've met me and we clicked. Right now, for me, it seems like some sort of magic has happened. But, Brad, we're both old enough to know that magic moments, most times, aren't enough to support a long-term relationship." She stopped.

What was she thinking? "You're right," he said. "We're still in one of those magic moments, and part of its magic has moved me off my indecisive butt to try to resolve my family situation. Right now, that's separate from you and me."

She was staring at him, so he felt the need to say more when silence might have been the better option. "I think we're off to a fantastic start in a relationship. But you're right. It's way too soon for us to even talk about anything past the weekend."

He should walk away, but he couldn't escape the conversational habit of a lifetime. "Even if you're not in my future, I still need to reinvent part of me so I can move on. Sorry, Kate, I'm not trying to scare you. Just wanted you to know what I'm thinking and planning."

He picked up his coat, laptop, and a folder.

She said nothing. Did she want the subject changed?

"My ride should be here any minute. Stay as long as you like. I'll be finished around four. I wrote my cell number on that pad. Call me about four-thirty. I can escape by then unless I get a business dinner invitation I can't avoid."

He leaned in to Kate and kissed her. He whispered, "You don't have to call me. I'll understand if you don't. But I do want to spend more time with you. A lot more time."

When he moved toward the door, she finally reacted by grabbing his arm. "Wait a minute. I have things to do, including going home to get out of these clothes. I'll be done by four o'clock, and I want to call you, and I want to pick you up, and I want to know more about you, and I'll kill anyone who invites you to dinner away from me. I'm taking you to dinner tonight." She took a deep breath.

He laughed. "How can I refuse an offer like that? See you later." Before he closed the door, he casually added, "Love you."

* * *

Kate's mind raced and her heart thumped, but this time it wasn't the lovemaking that caused it. Was that just a throw-away remark, or was there more to it? Everything seemed to be leading somewhere, but there were impossible roadblocks, even presuming she—and Brad—wanted the road to go somewhere.

She drank the last of the now-cold coffee. "Slow down, woman. Whatever happens, happens," she muttered and forced her mind to turn to things she had to do.

First, she needed to get home and change. To do that, she had to get her car back, which meant going to the lobby, still dressed in last night's clothes, to find out where it was. Earlier that morning, she'd rescued the balled-up leggings from her purse. She must look exactly what she was: a pick-up who'd spent the night with a hotel patron.

What about plan B? Phone the desk and see if she could collect the car from the hotel park. Or plan C: Ask if the car jockey could deliver it to the front door, enabling her to make a quick dash through the lobby when it arrived.

A call to the desk told her plan C could be activated whenever she was ready. She must get home. Enough of her situation with Brad and its potential possibilities and problems that she should put on the back burner. She had a daughter with a problem that needed sorting.

That same daughter was too astute. Kate must tell her about Brad, and maybe he and Jenny could meet the next day. These mother/daughter conversations didn't get any easier. And this upcoming one was directly out of left field. Then again, maybe it was too soon to say anything about a situation that probably had no future.

And how did her sixteen-year-old daughter know so much about sexual antics? Kate found it difficult to imagine their conversation, with her as the mother who had rediscovered sex. Maybe even romance.

She concluded that she could be in a role reversal if she confided in Jenny. Usually, it was the teenager telling the mother she'd found someone. The teenager was the confused individual needing advice and a safe shoulder to lean on.

She called the front desk to have her car brought to the door, stifling her laugh when the clerk replied, "Right away, Ms. Anderson."

She collected her belongings, checked herself in the mirror, took the elevator down, and tried to stroll confidently through the lobby, wondering if she looked like an escort who'd spent the night with her client. She hoped not and stared straight ahead, finally fixing her gaze on the grinning face of the same car jockey who'd parked the car the previous night.

"Any luggage, ma'am?"

Had he winked? *Screw this*, she thought, and firmly said, "No, I'm staying here again tonight."

She almost took his finger off when she closed the car door before he could.

Chapter 7
Updates and Secrets

8:40 a.m., Saturday, October 24th
Phone. Treetops Terrace, Kirkland, PQ, to the Halifax Conference Centre

As soon as Harry woke, he knew he had to talk to his father. His dad had always told him and James to call him, no matter when or where, if either of them had a problem. Harry had never felt the need to make such a call, but this was different. He didn't trust his mother and wasn't sure she had told the truth when she said his father knew all about that Aaron person.

Harry glanced at the clock. His mother would be asleep for at least another hour. His father had said the time was an hour later in Halifax and that his presentation was at ten o'clock Montreal time. Harry had to call right away, but he wasn't sure what he'd say. His father would know how to deal with the situation and would be home the next day to fix it. Harry had to tell him he knew what was happening and that his mother was spending all her time with Aaron. After a quick trip to the bathroom, he felt more alert. He found his cell phone, sneaked down the stairs to the kitchen, and speed-dialed his father.

* * *

Brad was backstage in the hotel auditorium doing a final review of his notes. The tech had promised the power point presentation was as planned and there would be no glitches. Brad needed another cup of coffee but couldn't risk needing the washroom halfway through the ninety minutes he'd been allotted. After presenting his information on the company's proposed wind farms, there would be questions and opposition. There always was, even if only from the NIMBY opponents. It was amazing how often Joe Public was in favour of alternate energy source exploitation until it came too close to home, even if there was no inconvenience.

His phone buzzed. Must remember to turn it off after this. He saw that it was Harry, so it must be important. He only ever rang in the evenings when Brad was away on business.

"What's up, son? Not like you to be up this early on a Saturday."

"I don't know where to start."

Brad waited for him to say something.

"Mom came home at two this morning. She said she was seeing this guy Aaron and that you knew about it. She said we'd all talk about it tomorrow when you got home and—"

Brad had to think fast. "I'm sorry you had to find out this way. Yes, I know about it. We could have told you, but we knew James couldn't deal with it, so we tried to keep it secret until it was the right time. James doesn't know anything, does he?"

"I don't know. He was asleep when Mom got home. But you could have told me. I wouldn't have told him. How could you do this to us?"

"Where's Mom now?" Brad asked.

"She's still in bed. She's probably not even going to talk to me when she gets up. I kinda told her off. But I don't care. How could you guys do this to us? And what are you going to do when you get home tomorrow?"

Off to one side, somebody said, "Five minutes, Mr. Anderson."

"Sorry, son. I have a presentation to make to about 300 people in a few minutes. We'll talk later. This isn't the end of the world. It's been coming for over a year. Please try to keep it a secret from James, at least until I get home on Monday. When I do get home, you, me, and Mom will sit down and talk."

"Monday? You're supposed to be home tomorrow!"

"I have to stay an extra night. Sorry, I can't avoid it."

The realization he had just lied to his already aggrieved and upset son was reinforced by a loud "Oh fuck, Dad."

There was no response when he attempted to reassure his seventeen-year-old that everything would work out.

* * *

"Who were you talking to like that?" His mother came down the stairs. Her blonde hair was tousled and her face unmade. She wore sweatpants and one of his dad's old T-shirts.

One day I'm going to post a photo of her looking like that on Facebook, he thought, *and she'll never be able to pass for thirty-something again.* He was certain she wasn't telling that Aaron creep her real age.

"Harry!" She raised her voice. "That wasn't your father, was it?"

"Yeah, it was. And I told him about the row we had last night, and he says he knew all about you and aarsole!"

"Come on, Harry! I don't need this. Please, let's try and talk sensibly." She sat on the bottom step and fluffed her hair. "What else did he say?"

"Not much because he was about to give his big presentation. But he said the three of us need to sit down and talk when he gets home. And that won't be until Monday. He has to stay over an extra night. Fuck! Don't either of you fucking care?"

"What! What's he thinking? He's needed here! I'm going to call him right back."

"You'll have to wait. He's busy, remember."

"Shit! That man! Always away when he should be here. Are you surprised that I—"

"Hey, James," Harry said, when he saw his younger brother on the top step. How long had he been there?

"Come on down, James," his mother said. "I'll get you some breakfast before I hit the shower."

To Harry, she whispered, "We'll have to be careful what we say to each other. And watch your language!"

"You too, Mom!"

Chapter 8
Wondering and Blundering

10:30 a.m., Saturday, October 24th
Treetops Terrace, Kirkland

James had just eaten two Pop-tarts washed down with orange juice when his mother entered the kitchen. Harry was almost finished his eggs and toast. He was slow because he was texting, non-stop.

"What are your plans for today? Anywhere you want to go? I can drop you off," she said.

"I'm meeting my friends at Fairview Mall at noon," Harry said.

"I'm going to Jean-Guy's." James had called Jean-Guy up the street earlier and was invited there for the day.

"I want you back by six," his mother said, looking directly at him. "You, too, Harry. I'm visiting Aunt Chrissie this evening."

"Is that right, Mom?" Harry said, in that funny, questioning way of his, which made James wonder what was going on.

She ignored Harry's question and rushed out of the kitchen. "Have to take a shower and get dressed."

Before going downstairs for breakfast, James had sat on the top step, not fully awake, listening to his mother and brother. Both had used bad language and seemed mad at his father.

Then the two pretended everything was okay, which made him aware something was wrong. With his mother out of the room, he decided if he wanted to know why Harry and his mom were mad at his father, he'd better ask his brother now.

* * *

Harry continued texting after his mother went upstairs because he didn't know what to say to his brother who, by now, should have been fully occupied playing a game or doing something in his room. Why was James staring at him? What had he heard before Harry spotted him listening from the staircase?

His worst fear was realized when his brother spoke. "Why are you and Mom mad at Dad?"

"Can't you see I'm busy? Ask me later. Or ask Mom."

"Did I hear you say he wasn't coming home until Monday?"

Avoidance tactic number two came to Harry, and he suggested it was time for James to get dressed and go to his friend's.

That one didn't work either. James, with increasing urgency in his voice, asked, "Why can't you tell me what's going on? Why's Mom mad at Dad, and why isn't he coming home tomorrow? What's wrong?"

Harry completed his text and placed his phone on the table. He finished his eggs and toast, slurped his coffee, and then looked over at his teary-eyed brother. What the hell should he say? He couldn't tell him what he thought he knew because he hadn't heard his father's version of events. But James needed an answer, or he'd keep at him.

Harry gave it his best shot. "Promise me you won't get upset."

His brother nodded.

"It's just that Mom and Dad aren't very happy with each other right now. Nothing to worry about. It'll sort itself out in time. It's just that things might get a bit tense around here. We'll all sit down sometime soon and sort things out."

Before James could come up with more questions and demand details, Harry added, "Oh, and please don't go asking Mom. She's not in the mood to answer questions right now, and she doesn't want you upset. Besides, we don't want to upset her any more, do we?"

"Like you did earlier!" his kid brother replied.

"Yes, James. Like I did earlier when I shouldn't have said some things I did. I promise you everything will be all right in the end. Now go and get ready. And don't forget your teeth."

James reluctantly, it seemed to Harry, headed up the stairs. Harry worried he'd said too much, but he also suspected his brother was old enough to hear more than a cover-up story. His mother was—what was the expression?—"overprotective."

James was so like their mom, with her blonde hair and slight build. The two of them were close, and Harry felt one of those fleeting pangs of jealousy that his mother had preferred James for as long as he could remember. But, given current events in her parenting, it didn't seem important anymore.

And then the "D" word came to the forefront of his over-speculative mind. What was going to happen to the two of them if it went as far as divorce? One positive would be less pressure from his mother for him to stay in Montreal at McGill or Concordia. Going to Dalhousie, or maybe Queens, would get him away from the upcoming turmoil. James would want to stay with his mother, but his father would demand a say in that. Things could turn into a mess.

Harry hoped his parents could find a solution because, as hard as he searched, he could find no answers.

* * *

James flung himself on the bed his mom must have straightened before she went in the shower. Harry was getting to be just like a grownup, never answering questions properly.

If James stayed with his mother instead of going to Jean-Guy's, she would tell him more. But Harry said they shouldn't upset her, so that wouldn't necessarily happen.

He was confused. What did Harry mean by "Everything will be all right in the end"? What "end"? What "things"?

What was happening between his parents? His mom was always out a lot—and not just selling houses. Sometimes she came home really late when his father was away.

He located his jeans and hockey shirt and began to organize his things to go to his friend's. Jean-Guy's mother always had lots of treats, and he liked going there.

When Dad gets home, James thought, *he and Mom can make things right at this house, too.*

Chapter 9
Appointment and Disappointment

11:00 a.m., Saturday, October 24th
Phone. West Condos, Clayton Park, Halifax, to Highway Condos, Bedford

Finally Kate could sit down in her own place. It was only about fifteen hours since she had left, but it seemed like a lifetime since she had been alone. She could have done some necessary shopping on the way home, but with all that was happening, routine stuff took a back seat. Except, of course, for the long relaxing shower and the change into something appropriate and not reminiscent of last night's out-of-character excursion.

Maybe that's all it was. Goodness knows she wouldn't be the first of her friends and acquaintances to dilly dally when separated or even, like her own sister, before separating. If it was a fling, whether a Friday night fling or a weekend wandering, she decided she could live with either. But she speculated it might develop beyond that. "Maybe I'm dreaming," she'd heard herself say in the shower.

While she enjoyed another coffee, with her feet up in her favourite chair, she realized it was time to phone her ex and arrange to meet with him. There was no way Mike and his bimbo's sexual high jinks should embarrass and upset Jenny on her weekends in Bedford with her father—irresponsible jerk that he was.

* * *

Mike reluctantly answered his cell. Suzie was performing her lengthy morning ritual, and Jenny had gone to meet friends at Sunnyside Mall. Mike hoped it wasn't work calling. He checked the number and then wished that it was work rather than his ex-wife. What the hell did she want this time? No phone call from her was ever good for him, or Suzie.

"Are you there? And don't you hang up on me!" Mike heard before he got a chance to speak.

"Don't get your knickers in a knot! What can I do for you this time? And don't even talk about more money. Suzie tells me those jeans and shirt will be around one fifty."

Mike knew that Kate had learned long ago not to react to him. Both knew that nothing constructive came if she did. It was too easy for them to argue.

She said she had something awkward to discuss with him and wondered if she could come to his condo around three o'clock, when Susie was out with Jenny.

His curiosity was aroused. "Why can't we talk about it on the phone?"

"Talk about what?" Suzie asked, emerging from the bathroom. Her loud voice would have carried to Kate.

"I don't know," Mike said, hoping Kate realized he was responding to Susie. When he said, "It's Kate. She wants to talk to me this afternoon when you're not here," he knew Kate must know Suzie was in the picture.

"Tell the bitch to leave you alone. No way are you meeting with her when I'm not around. Maybe she wants to jump your bones."

Any chance of continuing his conversation with Kate was gone. From Kate, he heard, "You still there, Mike? I know you can't talk with Suzie there. I'll drop by at three. It's important. And tell that Suzie I stopped jumping your bones years ago."

Mike said a pretend "goodbye" into the dead phone and waited for the onslaught.

"Well!" Suzie's voice at the best of times was grating and, when angry, was a total turn-off but impossible to ignore. "Is she coming? Because if she is, I'm not taking her kid shopping. She can stay here and we'll all three listen to what she wants. Maybe Jenny will hear how impossible her mother is and know why you walked out."

He was pleased that, after three months, Suzie still bought into that version of the separation that he'd spun. "No. She hung up when she heard you. I guess whatever is yanking her chain will have to wait." He continued his lies. "You go on your shopping trip, and don't forget to spend something on yourself. There's a game on TV that I can watch."

There was no response from his girlfriend, so he continued, "Can I make something for dinner, or shall we go out? Without Jenny, of course."

"Let me see." Suzie had calmed down. "Hmm, your cooking or a meal out with some drinks and dancing afterwards. And we both know what that leads to, don't we, lover?"

She sat on his lap and pondered his invitation. He was always amazed the only time Suzie's voice was sweet and gentle was when she felt sexy. That was, of course, in early arousal. The banshee returned as her sexual excitement increased. He postponed that possibility with a reminder that Jenny might be back any minute.

* * *

Kate sat back in her chair and tried to relax. Maybe once the divorce was final there would be no need to negotiate by phone about their daughter. And hopefully there'd be no more situations like the one she was going to try to sort out this afternoon.

Her mind meandered. As long as Mike was mixed up with women like Suzie, there would be more situations requiring Kate's common-sense solutions. God knows Mike showed few signs of maturing. How was he going to react when he found out about Brad? If there was anything to find out.

Chapter 10
Confirmation and Consternation

1:15 p.m., Saturday, October 24th
Phone from Treetops Terrace, Kirkland, PQ, to Conference Centre, Halifax

Jean-Guy's mother was clearing out a flowerbed in the front garden when Jill approached after dropping Harry at the mall. Jill should have made an attempt to get to know Mimi better, but it was too late now that the living situation for the Anderson family looked like it might change.

She stopped the car and wound down the window. "Hi, Mimi. Can you send James home by six at the latest?"

"Sure, no problem. The boys get along great, eh? No terrible teens yet." Mimi laughed.

"You're right." Jill had difficulty imagining James as a teen even though he'd just celebrated his thirteenth birthday. "Thanks for letting him stay so long. I should go. I have groceries to unload. We'll talk another time."

As Jill turned into her driveway, two doors away, she thought it would be best, in the long run, if she and the boys could stay here. Who knew if Aaron would want to move in right away. Maybe they'd keep the present arrangement for a while, with Jill in Kirkland making "social" visits to the Pointe Claire apartment while the boys gradually got to know Aaron.

She flung herself on the sofa and reached for her phone. Before she checked in with Aaron about the evening, she would call Brad to see why he couldn't get home until Monday. With both boys out of the house, she wouldn't have to watch what she said to him. Brad was never there when she needed him. It was the story of her married life.

Maybe she should tell it like it was and not mince words. She didn't need to be careful about twisting the truth, either.

And what exactly had Harry told his father? Guaranteed it was Harry's slant on the situation. And even more difficult to fathom, what version of marital history had Brad given to their son? She hoped she'd find out. Generally, she could still get the truth from her husband even though he knew she wasn't as truthful as she should be.

She smiled while she waited for him to answer the phone.

* * *

Brad was busy discussing his paper and his company while three people he did not know seemed to hang on every word. Two appeared to be students from the university, probably fulfilling the requirements of an assignment. The older man had introduced himself as belonging to the provincial Department of Energy, though at what level he hadn't revealed. When his cell rang, Brad was glad of an excuse to escape.

"I'm sorry, I have to take this," he lied when Jill's number appeared.

He wandered toward a quiet corner of the room where the buffet lunch had been served. He knew the advantage of getting in the first words with her on the phone. "Before you say anything, you should know that Harry called me early this morning and told me about the confrontation at two this morning. That must have ruined your evening."

"You should have been here. If you had been, it wouldn't have happened."

He didn't take the bait, and she relayed what she had said to Harry in response to his accusations. Not sure he was hearing the truth, Brad told her he had told their seventeen-year-old that he was aware of the Aaron situation. "I told him changes were inevitable. His main questions dealt with what, when, and how. We also discussed how to explain the situation to James. I told him not to tell him anything until I got home."

She warned she had other things that Brad might not like to hear but agreed it was time to look at their situation.

He grunted an affirmative and waited for the accusations he was sure were forthcoming.

There seemed to be a note of glee in her voice when she informed him of her belief that his favourite son, Harry, was even angrier at his father than he was at her.

"I find that hard to believe."

"Well, how about this one?" Jill said. "I strongly suspect that James has some inkling about what's going on. I think we can only stall him for a little while longer before he starts asking questions. We should be ready for that."

Brad saw what was coming from the conniving bitch who knew how to set him up. She'd laid the table and had picked up the carving knife! He quickly went on the offensive. "I expect Harry told you I'm hung up here at our office on Monday. I won't be home until about seven. Can you keep James in the dark until then?"

"Damn you, Brad!" Jill screamed. "What's more important to you? Your two sons and the future of our family or that job that keeps you away whenever something important is happening back here? It's no fucking wonder I prefer time with Aaron to time with you."

Brad was leaning against the wall, scared to hold the phone too far away in case someone in the busy lunchroom heard him taking abuse. Some of it was deserved, but he had no chance to break in and answer the accusations.

She finished with an emphatic "So, what are you going to do?"

He almost reacted by saying he'd be home on Sunday.

"Nothing to say?" Jill's anger broke the protracted silence.

"I can't promise, but I'll see what I can do about getting home tomorrow. But whenever I get home, we will talk and get this separation going. Agreed?"

He waited for another earful, which was relatively mild.

"I'm pissed at you, Brad. But at least we agree on a separation. The sooner we talk about it, the better." She cut the call off.

A work colleague stood by the door, probably looking for him. Dragging his mind back to the conference, he walked over to meet him.

* * *

Jill flung her phone hard into the opposite armchair. She was thankful that her aim, in anger, was good. She got up to retrieve it. She needed to talk to Aaron. She could escape this domestic mess for a few hours this evening, and then, perhaps, a little afternoon delight the next day. She could always pretend she was helping a fellow agent with an open house. Goodness knows that alibi had worked more than a few times already.

She punched in Aaron's number, but he didn't pick up.

Men! So unreliable, especially when you need them for comfort and joy.

Chapter 11
Evasion by Recreation

3:00 p.m., Saturday, October 24th
Phone from Treetops Terrace, Kirkland, to 5729 rue de Bienville, Montreal

Jill tried to call Aaron again. So much for a restful afternoon alone at home. If Aaron would return her calls or respond to her texts, she could relax. She had been trying to contact him for over two hours. Her mind went into the "what-ifs," and with Aaron, that was always "What if he's with some other woman?" Then she'd veer to: "Is he back chasing younger women—those young girls in the pubs and lunch bars in town?"

He'd once said that a Saturday lunch, lasting through the afternoon, was prime pickup time. Maybe he was up to his old tricks again, running around on her.

She tried yet again. Straight to voice mail, but she didn't leave another message, Four was enough. Even that many gave off a strong odour of anxiety.

* * *

Aaron was alone in a strange bed when he woke sufficiently to wonder where he was. Why was he in a small bed? Who was in the shower behind the half-closed door? He looked at his wrist to check the time, but he wasn't wearing his watch. Light streamed in through the glass doors that led to a balcony.

Gradually, he recalled the events of the small hours of Saturday morning. He'd been greeted at the apartment door by a naked Sophia, who was either half-drunk or stoned—or both. Goodness knew what she was on, for she was certainly more awake and aroused than he was. But it took her very little time and effort to get his arousal level sufficient to perform.

He didn't remember falling asleep. In a recovery moment between the gymnastic eroticism, Sophia had produced her stash. Partaking of that must have increased the insatiable lust in her. Eventually, he had to plead satiation.

He hoped it was Sophia in the shower. Who else would it be? The bedroom was certainly female, but with clothing strewn around, it didn't look like the candle-lit room he'd been welcomed into in the wee hours.

Before he could investigate further, a phone vibrated on the wood floor by the bed. He scrambled for it and saw it was his. It was Jill.

Aaron didn't answer. Instead, he checked messages. Jill had called four times and left several texts. He needed a shower and a coffee before he could talk to her and come up with a believable story as to why he hadn't answered his phone. And that couldn't be done in Sophia's company. *I've got a live one here,* Aaron thought. *It may be a very young live one, but it's too soon to throw her back into the pool.*

His phone showed that it was past three in the afternoon.

With just a towel wrapped round her, Sophia appeared from the shower. She seemed even younger in her almost state of undress. He wondered which year she was in at U de M and quickly erased the thought that he was old enough to be her father.

When she saw he was awake, she padded over to the bed and, without a greeting, let the towel drop and flung her arms round his neck. Her breasts brushed against his chest. She kissed him but cut it short. "Aaron, you stink. Your breath is atrocious. There's a spare toothbrush in the bottom drawer in the bathroom. And get a shower, too. That sexy male odour last night is now over-ripeness." She grinned. "But you still turn me on. I'll be here waiting."

When Aaron ignored her and headed to the bathroom to answer the urgent messages from his bladder, Sophia shouted, "I can get dressed if you want. Then you can tell me all about this Jill who has phoned you three times and wonders where you are."

Aaron turned. "You stay just the way you are. And Jill is this older woman who is harassing me and won't leave me alone." He feared the worst and smiled his most reassuring smile. "Did you speak to her?"

Sophia laughed. "Course not, silly. Just picked it up when it buzzed and read the screen. Can't trust these cougars. They either want a young stud or a husband. And you could fit in either category, so hurry back, stud."

While enjoying the shower, Aaron, again reminded by young Sophia's comments, came to the conclusion that Jill viewed him as husband material. Their relationship was becoming perilously close to something semi-permanent. To a woman like Jill, the next step was either moving in together or a formal engagement. No! Jill had to go. If she didn't, how could he continue to pull pieces like Sophia?

He wrapped a towel around his waist and used Sophia's deodorant and toothpaste. Still damp, with the tousled look that subtracted years from him, he returned to bed where the seductive Sophia lay. Her body personified afternoon delight.

Aaron's last thought was that he'd find an opportunity to call Jill later and give her the fond farewell. And then Sophia began the process of reassuring him he'd made the right decision. And she didn't have to say a word.

* * *

"Where the hell is he?" Jill muttered for the umpteenth time. "Who is he with, and what the hell is he doing? I don't know why I bother. He's just too much grief. Can I trust him? No! Do I need him? No!"

That last answer was a lie. Well, not exactly. She didn't "need" him. But God almighty, she wanted him and couldn't live without him. A tear rolled down her cheek toward the wine glass that needed refilling.

She vowed she wouldn't phone again—at least not until just before it was time for the boys to come home, say 5:30. Surely Aaron would have called or at least texted before then. She and Aaron were due to spend the evening together, though she couldn't stay out as late as she did the previous night. She was sure if she went out, Harry would be waiting up again.

Jill set down her empty wine glass, deciding she should stop drinking if she was going out that evening. Besides, she had the boys to feed. And a talk with Chrissie would be good since she usually handed out excellent advice.

But first, there was time for a catnap. She needed sleep almost as much as she needed Aaron.

Chapter 12
Request and Recriminations

3:30 p.m., Saturday, October 24th
Highway Condominiums, Bedford

Kate had said three o'clock. Mike glanced at his watch. Just like her to be late. What the hell was the problem this time? He looked forward to the day when his divorce would be finalized. Maybe then he'd tell her where to go if she still kept making demands on him.

He prayed Suzie wouldn't come home early, but maybe it would be good for Jenny to see her mom, the control freak, putting him down. Further reflection brought him back to reality and self-preservation. If Suzie knew Kate had been here when Suzie wasn't, the younger woman would be pissed, and Mike wanted to avoid that at all costs.

Time for another beer. He'd just taken the first swig when the buzzer sounded.

"You're late, but come up anyway," he said through the intercom. He chugged the rest of the beer and moved the four empty bottles into the kitchen just when the tap sounded on the door.

Here we go again, he thought, opening the door.

* * *

"Sorry, I'm late," Kate said, but she didn't waste her breath making excuses. Mike looked a mess. Had he showered yet? And didn't that Suzie woman know how to use the washer and dryer? She certainly had no idea what an iron was for, if Mike's crumpled appearance was anything to go by.

As Kate edged through the door, she smelled a whiff of beer beneath the remnants of cigarette smoke. Mike didn't seem to have cut down on the smoking and drinking. And the condo wasn't exactly clean.

He indicated a chair and, as he sat opposite her, asked, "What is it this time, Kate? If you keep this up, I'll have to ask you to go through my lawyer. Every week it's something. This is close to harassment."

She'd calmed down before she got out of the car in the condo parking lot, but one short speech from this excuse for a man and she was ready for another battle of words. Couldn't he see that some things were easy to settle without going through a lawyer? Why was he always on the attack when it would be much simpler to sit and discuss?

Here goes, she thought. *However I say this will just be more shit hitting the fan to him.*

Calmly, she told him about the early morning phone call from Jenny and how their daughter was embarrassed by the sounds coming from the other bedroom. "She doesn't even want to come here anymore with all that going on."

He looked bemused. Kate wasn't sure if he was lying when he said, "I don't understand."

"Do I have to spell it out, Mike? It seems your girlfriend is a screamer and her pillow shouting is not what an innocent sixteen-year-old should be exposed to. Can you and Suzie show a little restraint when Jenny's here, please?"

He got up out of the chair and, as he turned his back to look out the window, she heard, "Fuck! That's enough. Now you want to control how I make love to other women?"

He faced her. Past experience told her he was angry, and if the past was any indication, who knew what would come out of his mouth.

"I might expect something like that from a frigid bitch like you. You will never understand passion and the sheer enjoyment of sex. Maybe our daughter will if she hears it coming from our bed."

Kate's thoughts swung back to the previous night at the hotel with Brad, but no way would she bring up that to argue her case.

"What I have with Suzie is something special, and part of that is throwing care and inhibition aside. But you wouldn't understand. And even if you did, you'd never want to lose control, would you?"

Once again, she was tempted to rebut his condemnation. Instead, she tried to continue the simple message she had brought.

"Mike, I'm not trying to tell you and Suzie how to run your love life, but when Jenny is here, can you keep it down a bit? And while you're at it, whatever you watch on TV or the computer, keep the volume lower, please. I don't think I'm asking too much for the two weekends a month that Jenny visits. I'm doing my best to push her toward you. You're her father, and I think Suzie likes Jenny. She's like a big sister to her."

She stopped, not wanting to step over the divorcing-parents boundary, but couldn't stop herself from adding, "How old is she, anyway?" As soon as the question came out, she regretted it, anticipating the explosion that would ensue.

"She's twenty-one, as if that's any business of yours. You're forty, going on sixty! She's alive. You're on my retired list. I'm lucky to have her, and sometimes I wonder why she's with me. I'll do anything to keep her. You stay out of my life. You tried to run it for twenty years and now I've escaped. So, before you have any more suggestions of how I should live my life, you can leave."

She remained still. "What should I tell Jenny?"

"I don't care what you tell her, but she needs to know that not all homes are quiet and controlled like yours is. Oh, I can't wait to tell Suzie about your latest move. Fuck, Kate. She'll be even more pissed off than I am."

She'd heard enough. She gathered her coat and purse. When she reached the door, she turned, wanting the final comment. "Can I expect your bratty girlfriend on my doorstep ready to scratch my eyes out? She'll never grow up, and you seem to be getting younger every time we talk. Not in looks, either! And I don't want my daughter exposed to porn with her father as a participant, thank you."

She slammed the door and took the stairs rather than waiting for the elevator. She didn't need her angry ex abusing her while she waited.

* * *

Mike wanted to throw something or, better still, hit Kate. Why on earth did he marry that woman? How had he stuck it out for—what was it?—eighteen years? Must have been those bits on the side that kept him sane. But none of those women matched what he had with Suzie. So what if she was almost half his age. He could still keep up with her.

He calmed down as he thought about his lover. What a body. And, other than when in bed, she made no demands of him. Every day, she found a reason to say, "I can't wait until your divorce is final."

The only time Suzie asked for money was for groceries even though she liked to eat out a lot. She dressed up when they went out for dinner and even looked good heading for work at the call centre. She sometimes complained when he said they couldn't afford to go to a club on a weekend, but she understood a portion of his money had to go to Kate as support for Jenny. He hoped they could soon take that trip to Cape Breton so he could meet her parents and family. It would be good to do that before winter set in.

Grabbing another beer from the fridge, he turned his attention to the more immediate problem. How would he tell Suzie about Jenny's complaint without admitting that Kate had been in the condo while she was out?

Chapter 13
Contact and Continuation

4:30 p.m., Saturday, October 24th
Phone from West Condos, Clayton Park, to Halifax Convention Centre

During the short drive back home, Kate thought of so many ways she could have approached Mike about Jenny's difficulty with the graphic sounds and uninhibited language coming through the bedroom walls. She convinced herself that however she had approached the subject, he would have reacted the same way, for he had never understood the concept of diplomacy. He was probably the most inconsiderate man she knew, which was what finally forced their separation—that and the string of other women Kate had eventually discovered when one of them called one evening when Mike was out.

With his typical lack of consideration, he had dumped the wrong one. This particular one—oh, what was her name?—had decided Mike's wife could exact revenge for both of them. Kate's initial reaction had been to slam the door on the ridiculous pointy toes of those "fuck me" high-heeled shoes worn by the over-made-up Jolene. Yes, Jolene—that was her name.

But beneath all that makeup was an obvious nervous wreck, whose announcement, "I'm one of your husband's girlfriends—or I was," preceded a tear that tracked though the mascara.

"You'd better come in" was an invitation that had started Kate toward her new life. Much later, when Mike walked through the door of their condominium, he found a packed suitcase inside the door. After he remonstrated and pleaded with her when discovering how much she knew, he'd noticed Sean, her brother, the city policeman, standing at the other end of the room.

When Mike had begun his excuses as a prelude to an explanation riddled with lies, she'd told him not to waste his breath. She had names and had had enough. Sean had then intervened and told him to go. He'd escorted Mike and his baggage to the car. Kate didn't know the message Sean gave Mike, but her brother had succeeded in keeping Mike away from her. She had agreed to Sean's order: "Call me if Mike is ever a problem."

While she parked, her mind switched to the decision she'd been avoiding. It was past four, and she wanted to phone Brad. She didn't care about anything beyond Monday. She wanted to see him and spend as much time as she could with him.

* * *

Brad looked at his watch. She had said four o'clock, hadn't she? Maybe she had decided against seeing him again. He couldn't blame her if she had. He had enough baggage, sufficient to put off any woman, if he told her the truth, which he had.

The conference was finished for the day. Most participants were en route to their homes or hotels or headed to a bar to begin their evening's relaxation. He was sure his presentation had been well received. There had been a lively question and answer session, after which he felt he had appeased the opponents of the suggested wind farms. The weekend had been a success, even if Friday night ended up being happenstance followed by regret. The regret certainly wasn't coming from him. He wanted to see where the night might lead. He needed to hear from Kate.

He willed his phone to ring. With his luck, if it rang it would be Jill or one of the boys with another addition to the complexity of his Kirkland life. He'd give Kate until five. He would have a drink while he waited

Half-way to the bar, his phone vibrated in his pocket. One look and he almost danced a jig in the lobby.

Before Kate had a chance to say anything, Brad gabbled, "Oh, am I ever glad that it's you. I don't care if you're late. You called, and I want you to have dinner with me and to spend the evening with me, and before you come to the hotel it would be wonderful if you brought a tote—an overnight bag—because we have so much to talk about—"

"Slow down, Brad! Slow down!"

He stopped to think of what he had said and his pessimistic side told him he had blown it. Kate was doing the right thing for her and was phoning to say, "Thanks, but no more. It's over."

Instead, she asked, "Where are you?"

"Still at the conference centre. Why?"

"Well, if I don't know where you are, how can I find you? And I do want to find you."

Brad had to sit. He found a chair and said, "You do say the sweetest things, Kate. Where do you want to meet? I can take a taxi to the hotel or a restaurant or wherever. Right now I could probably fly to see you."

Kate laughed. "I'll pick you up at the main entrance of the convention centre at . . ."

He realized she was checking the time.

"Ah, it's quarter to five now. I'll pack a bag, get changed, and drive over to pick you up at six. Watch for my car. I'll stop when I see you and you can hop in. We can go back to the hotel, you can . . ."

There was another pause. "Oh, I'm over-organizing something that should be spontaneous."

"There is a danger of that." He laughed and hoped she heard the humour in his voice. "Let's get to the hotel and take it from there, though it should include dinner sometime, somewhere. I'll grab a drink here and make it last until six when I'll be at the door looking for you. Oh, and Kate, thanks."

"As long as it's what we both want."

He heard the cautious side of this enticing woman, who was obviously uncertain of passing events.

"It's what I want," he said. "Now go get ready. Can't wait to see you again."

* * *

I'm just like a teenager, Kate thought, as she threw her phone on the bed. *Going to get all gussied up for a date that I know is going to be an all-nighter. I've set myself an impossible time deadline. I can't be late, and I have no idea what's happening beyond tonight. Who is this woman? What is she doing with her life? Why is she so excited?*

These questions about herself were beyond her comprehension. She laughed, realizing she was, indeed, acting like a teenager. She thought back to when she was sixteen. *Do it and worry about it later. But you know there's not going to be anything to worry about. Cos you're sixteen!*

She recalled the cover-up lies and half-truths that went with sixteen-year-olds' spontaneity and impetuous actions. She was an adult, and adult relationships didn't need lies, but they did have consequences. But to hell with it, she thought. *Let's be sixteen again!*

Kate laughed at this strange persona inhabiting her mind and body while she went from the "over-thinking" to the "doing," which started with turning on the shower. Usually, she did a lot of pondering in the shower, where the comforting water cleansed her. But she had too much to do to get ready for her date.

Back in reality, she believed she could do this, and if it went nowhere, she would have enjoyed the experience. As she luxuriated, she realized how much she wanted Brad. The only problem was that she wanted more than his intriguing and exciting physical presence. She wanted much more of the whole Brad.

Her mind switched after she turned off the shower. “So much to do and so little time” became her credo for the next thirty minutes of this different life that might end the next day.

Chapter 14
Doubts and Discomfort

5:00pm, Saturday, October 24th
In Suzie's car en route to Highway Condos, Bedford

Jenny wanted to thank Suzie, yet again, for the jeans and top even though they were spending her dad's money. Shopping was fun with Suzie. Suzie had also paid for a makeover but walked away afterward without buying any of the expensive cosmetics that were being promoted.

Instead, they'd gone farther down the mall to another store, where Suzie had insisted Jenny buy various products from a friend who worked there. When Jenny said she couldn't afford them, Suzie had flashed her dad's credit card. She laughed when Jenny pointed out that the jeans and top had exceeded the allowable budget. "What does a man expect when he gives you his credit card and sends you off shopping? You'll learn soon enough, Jenny."

While Suzie made the slow drive up the misleadingly named Bedford Highway, Jenny looked at the smiling woman and thought again, *It's like being with an older sister.* But then her mind flashed back to the words she'd heard coming through the bedroom walls from her "sister's" mouth the previous night. One day she'd ask her about that. Her mom wasn't easy to talk to about that stuff, but she envied her friends who had older sisters who shared information and issued warnings, which moms did. But moms didn't always tell you what to expect from boys—what was allowable, and definitely not what was pleasurable and exciting and unwise or even dangerous.

Jenny bet that Suzie could tell her a lot about sex and how to keep it secret from her parents. There had to be more to it than the stuff found on the internet. "Ronnie with the rotten reputation" claimed to be something of an expert, though some of Jenny's friends said he was all talk and no action. No way was Jenny giving Ronnie the chance to share his expertise, even in words.

Her mind took a half turn when she realized that whatever Suzie could be persuaded to tell her would be what she experienced with Jenny's father. Ugh. Gross.

She hoped that her parents had talked in the afternoon so she wouldn't have to listen to that . . . that—she didn't know what to call it—again this evening.

* * *

I had a good time this afternoon, even if I didn't buy much for me, Suzie thought, stopped at yet another traffic light on the crawl home. *I like being with this kid. Never been close to a younger sister. Boy, the things I could teach her, or warn her about, if I wasn't with her father.*

There was only a five-year difference in their ages. She wondered how different Jenny would be in five years. Jenny seemed so innocent. Suzie's innocence had disappeared around that age. She and Chuck had moved to Halifax, supposedly to find work. What would her parents say if they knew the real reason she had left home was for an abortion. She couldn't have had one in Glace Bay without the world knowing about it and suffering all sorts of repercussions.

Suzie wondered where Chuck ended up. Last she heard, he was headed to Alberta.

Mike was always pestering her about meeting her family. That might be difficult, for her mother had never forgiven her once Rose, her big sister, had blabbed about the abortion. Last time she'd been home, her mother had barely spoken to her. Maybe she'd go home for Christmas, but not with Mike though she'd love to show him off to family and friends. There would be comments about him being too old for her. She wondered about that herself. It was hard, sometimes, to resist the temptation to spend time with her own age group, especially when Mike didn't feel like going out or used the excuse he couldn't afford it.

Perhaps next summer. She needed to mend fences before daring to take him home to meet her family.

At the next light, where the intersection was log-jammed, she turned to Jenny, whose head was against the headrest and her eyes closed. On impulse, she asked, "Do you think I'm too young for your father?"

It was not surprising that Jenny was unresponsive to the change in topic. Up to then, they'd discussed mundane issues, such as shopping and tastes in music.

Jenny's eyes finally opened, and she looked across at Suzie. "Why do you ask that?"

"Oh, I don't know. Just wondered. Does he ever talk to you about me? I sometimes think he's too old for me."

"No, he never talks about you."

Suzie went on. "Like, sometimes I want to be out with people my own age, you know, just hanging out. Then there are times when your dad and I are so good for each other. Then there's times when we seem like an old married couple, never going anywhere or doing anything. I get so antsy. Sorry, I shouldn't have asked you." She stopped talking when the traffic moved.

"You sure sounded restless in bed last night. The things you were saying."

Suzie felt her face turn red. "I'm sorry." She drove toward the entrance to the condos and added, "Oh, that's just sex. I can get that anywhere. But your dad is good in bed!"

* * *

Jenny was happy when the car pulled into the garage and stopped, as did the conversation, which was becoming increasingly uncomfortable. She hadn't liked it when Suzie questioned her and asked for advice. Big sisters gave advice; they didn't ask for it.

In the elevator, Jenny hoped the conversation wouldn't continue in the apartment, especially if her father was there. She figured one day Suzie would walk out on her father and wondered if he had any inkling about his girlfriend's doubts.

"Jenny, don't tell your father or mother what I said, eh?"

Jenny glanced at Suzie. "Sure, no problem."

Her father was home. They showed off their purchases. Suzie insisted Jenny model the jeans and top. She did so but was uncomfortable noticing how her father eyed her. She wasn't a baby any longer.

Suzie confessed they had gone over budget. He was surprisingly understanding about the fifty dollar overspend. It was only after the three settled down to the pizza he'd ordered, that Jenny understood why.

He shared with them that her mother had visited. That was when all hell broke loose.

Jenny waited for Suzie to calm down before she called her mother, who wasn't answering her phone.

Chapter 15
Forsaken and Forlorn

5:40 p.m., Saturday, Oct 24th
Phone from Treetops Terrace, Kirkland, to 5729 rue de Bienville, Montreal

Still nothing from Aaron. Where was he? Who was he with? Jill's mind worked overtime. Maybe there was a hockey game. He could be at the Bell Centre.

More than two hours had passed since she last tried him. With one, if not both, of her sons knowing something strange was happening in the family, she had to be cautious. The boys were due back any minute. She should try again before they came home.

She rationalized her need to contact her lover. That would be all she needed: that part of her life to fall apart. Maybe that was his game for the day. Ignore her and she'd go away.

Please God, make him pick up. I need to hear his voice. I need to talk to him. Please be there, Aaron.

At least it was ringing.

An accented female voice said, "Mr. Drapkin's room. He can't come to the phone right now. He's in the shower, and I'm about to join him." A giggle and then Aaron's background voice. "You stupid cow. Give me that phone!"

What the hell was going on?

More female laughter and that same girlish voice with the francophone accent saying, "You said she had to go. I'm only trying to help."

* * *

Aaron made an instant decision when he snatched the phone from Sophia. There was no way he could talk himself out of this situation. Time to make a clean break. Someone as accomplished as he was in the manipulation of women's affections might be able to salvage something. His mind spun.

She wants me, he thought, *but does she want me enough to just play around now and again?*

Jill screamed, “Is that you, Aaron? What the hell is going on? Who was that? Talk to me!”

He took a deep breath and spoke words he said often. “I can explain, Jill.” But he knew he couldn’t and that he wouldn’t get a chance to try if the near hysteric on the other end of the line didn’t shut up.

“Where are you? You’re in some hotel room with some tart you’ve picked up, aren’t you? I thought we were going out tonight! What the fuck, Aaron! Who is she?”

Jill must have heard him the fourth time he tried to cut her off with her name. Quickly, before she drew breath and restarted, he jumped in. “I’m at home,” he lied.

The lies continued. Sophia was an old friend, and they’d met up when he went to the Trocadero for lunch. A few of his friends had come back with him, and they were reminiscing about old times. “We used to play jokes to embarrass each other. And that’s what we were doing when she answered the phone.”

“Put her on then, Aaron, so she can tell me the same lies you just told me.”

The shower was running in Sophia’s bathroom. Even if she was available, she couldn’t, and probably wouldn’t, confirm Aaron’s alibi.

The excuse, “She’s in the bathroom,” was uttered without conviction and only encouraged Jill’s need for confirmation of his story.

“Let me talk to another of these friends that came back to your place. And why didn’t you return my texts and calls? We’re supposed to be going out this evening, aren’t we?’

The tone of her voice and the speed of her diction increased.

He had to say his piece or he’d never get a chance. “She’s taking a shower, and I wasn’t exactly truthful when I said we came back here with friends. She—”

Before he could cover his half lie with others, the hysterical Jill launched into it again.

“You’ve been fucking, haven’t you? A little afternoon delight, was it? Were you going to bed her, change the sheets, and then expect me to be dessert later today? Well, screw you, you prick. I hope you realize what you’re throwing away. I hope she’s worth it, but an easy pickup like that skanky whore could never be . . .” Jill dissolved into tears that washed away coherent speech.

Irretrievable was Aaron’s opinion as he contemplated ending the call, but he saw an opportunity while she was vulnerable. “I’m sorry, Jill. It just happened, and she is an old friend, but I should have thought this through. But you know me. Don't always think with the head on my shoulders."

All Aaron could hear from Jill were sobs and snuffles. He took the opportunity to continue. Time for the truth, he reasoned. My version of the truth, anyway.

"But I have been using my brain, Jill. It tells me that we are getting too intense and exclusive in our relationship. You know I can never be exclusive. I believe we should cool it for a while, and maybe look at ourselves in a few weeks to see what's there and see if I really matter more than Brad and the kids—"

He knew he'd gotten the correct message across when Jill exploded with, "Fuck you, Aaron. You are such a conniving, lying, two-faced bastard. I don't know why I was in love with you. Go join your skank in the shower. You both need to clean up your act. I hate you!"

The line went dead. As Sophia came out of the bathroom, wrapped in a towel totally and purposefully inadequate as a cover-up, she asked, "C'est fini?"

"Merci a toi, Sophia, elle est fini."

* * *

Jill was thankful she'd called Aaron from her bedroom. Harry and James would be home any minute. They'd be hungry but would have to wait. Not sure whether she was angry or devastated, or a combination of both, she raced downstairs. Tears dripped off her nose while she wrote a note to the boys saying she was soaking in the bath.

While she filled the tub, the tears continued. She gazed at her naked self in the bathroom mirror, telling herself that, for her age, her body was inviting, and once the invitation was accepted, it only got better.

Sinking into the soothing water, she mumbled, "So, if that's the case, why couldn't I keep Aaron?"

From there, her thoughts turned even more negative, culminating in the unanswerable, "What do I do now?"

Fortunately, an announcement from the other side of the bathroom door, "We're home, Mom. What's to eat?" brought her back to the present.

"Give me half an hour and I'll be down to fix a meal. Find something to snack on if you're starving."

The question that needed a positive answer was whether she could get herself together in thirty minutes because, as Brad often said, "Life goes on."

Chapter 16
Fast and Fearful

7:45 p.m., Saturday, October 24th
Historic Properties Hotel, Halifax

"If I wasn't hungry before, I sure am now," Brad said, rolling to the left side of the bed.

Kate thought it funny they hadn't discussed beforehand which side of the bed belonged to whom, but comments later revealed that, in the life from which they were seeking escape, their respective partners had occupied the same spaces. Unless, Kate mused, Brad had been too polite to say otherwise, not wanting to ask to change sides.

Time would tell. Or would it? Would this last long enough to sort out and accommodate preferences? And not just in bed, because on this visit, comfort had not been an issue until now.

"We should eat. You had lunch, but all I got was coffee and a muffin at Tim's. I'm ravenous," Kate said, decorously pulling the duvet over her chest. "Do you want to go out? There are some good restaurants we can walk to."

"Did you say 'ravenous' or 'ravishing'?" Before she had a chance to answer, he added, "I think I've been both since we got here."

She laughed.

They had made small talk on the short drive to the hotel. She had walked through the lobby on Brad's arm. In the other, he carried his briefcase and her tote. She didn't feel any more comfortable crossing the busy lobby because it was her third time, but she was no longer self-conscious. She felt good, and she felt "right." She couldn't explain the feeling, but even if her liaison with Brad could be condemned, her actions were "right." There was no other word for them.

When they had found themselves alone in the elevator, the embrace and kiss seemed natural. There was passion in both, but it was not blatantly sexual. Had they been sharing the elevator, the hug would have waited until the door of room 8023 closed behind them. As it was, once the door closed, they were all over one another until she felt the bed behind her knees and collapsed, dragging him with her.

The passion had turned to a sexual hunger. They clumsily helped each other undress and made love on top of the bed. That hunger, which had grown in each of them after they reconnected, had been temporarily satisfied.

* * *

Brad did not dare suggest a room service dinner. Despite the fact they had flung their clothes everywhere, Kate's clothes showed she had gone to great pains to dress up for him. Whether the dress and presentation were recoverable was a question only she could answer.

"If you don't want to go out again, we could eat at the restaurant here. Do you know anything about it?" He asked.

"It's got a good reputation, but it's very pricey. And remember, dinner is my treat. I promised."

He had his answer. "I won't hold you to that since I'm on an expense account and can charge you as a client. What say we eat here? I hope you can put that outfit back together after I just about tore the dress off you." He chuckled. "Sorry about that."

"The dress doesn't crease. But saying that I'm a chargeable client makes me sound like a call girl. Really, Mr. Anderson," she smirked, "what sort of woman do you think I am?"

She scrambled from the tangled duvet, reached for her dress, shook it out, and posed with it held in front of her. As she sashayed to the bathroom and her unencumbered rear retreated, he marvelled at his luck.

Restored and sedate, they took the elevator to the Starlight Restaurant overlooking the now-illuminated harbour. Over dinner, Brad took the opportunity to tell her of his conversation with his wife. Kate seemed happy he had arranged to spend an extra night in Halifax.

"But the best bit is that Jill and I talked about getting a separation agreement on the table when I get home. By Monday, she should have gotten over being pissed off with me, and we should be able to talk realistically and begin to sort it out."

He waited for a reaction while Kate dabbed her lips with her napkin. She seemed to have lost interest in her pasta after he'd shared his two pieces of news.

"Say something. I told you I'd decided to do this. Now Jill agrees that it's time."

Kate picked up her fork and played with her linguine. "So how come she's pissed off at you?"

"I don't know. Probably because I initiated it and not her. Probably she wanted to decide when James, our youngest, was ready to deal with it. She was always at me to be more decisive. Now, when I am, she's pissed."

* * *

"I need to understand your wife a bit more, and I have some other questions," Kate said, "but let's talk back in the room where it's private." This needed sorting, but a hotel dining room was not the place to pose these sorts of questions.

She was thankful that Brad, recognizing if not understanding her discomfort, agreed. He changed the subject and asked what she'd done with her day. Over dessert and the last of the wine, they laughed as she explained her visit to her ex to talk about his rowdy sexual activity that had so disturbed her daughter.

After Brad signed the bill and they left the restaurant, she said, "I guess my ex is even more pissed off at me than your wife is at you. I'd love you to make me understand how your decisions today are still good even though they've angered your wife."

The conversation continued in the elevator they shared with two elderly couples. Brad and Kate clasped hands at chest level, facing each other. She wondered what the other couples were thinking when two people, so obviously enamored of one another, discussed the wife of the predatory male. That's how Brad would be perceived, she was sure, by those oldies.

When they reached the door of room 8023, Kate said, "No ravishing until we've had a talk, Brad."

"You're beginning to sound like my wife, Ms. Hull."

She unlocked the door, and Brad launched onto the queen-sized bed.

"Funny you should mention her, Mr. Anderson," she said, sitting demure and cross-legged in the armchair. "As a legitimate, chargeable expense, I have my scale of fees. The cost of me joining you on that bed are answers to a couple of questions."

"I agree even though I think your fees are high."

She was pleased Brad played along with her, trying to lighten the seriousness of the situation.

She needed to know one fact. "Please tell me that Jill isn't angry because you told her about us and last night."

Brad sat up, leaning back on his elbows. "I may be acting a lot out of character, but I'm a long way from being crazy. Of course I said nothing about us. I still see you and me as a situation not connected to Jill and me separating. Though that's becoming increasingly difficult."

"Full marks for that answer, Mr. Anderson. Question number two: If this weekend is getting in the way of your home life and decisions you need to make, would you like me to leave?"

"I said it's difficult, not impossible. I'm legally separating from and eventually divorcing Jill. I want you to stay, but only if you want to. Remember, if I loved her, you would never have been in this room with me." Brad appeared deadly serious.

Kate believed he wasn't trying to hide anything, so she continued in a more serious vein. "Are we going too fast and too far this weekend? With no fixed destination?"

"Can I answer your question with one of my own? You're here, but do you see any future for us beyond Monday's goodbye when I go to the airport?"

She blurted out, "Like you, I'm not sure. Maybe there will be more, maybe there won't. This is an adventure. You're not the only one acting out of character. I almost don't believe I'm behaving this way this weekend. I want to stay. I want to stay all night. I want time with you tomorrow and Monday. Right now, I hope there will be something beyond, but I also know you could be spinning me a long, elaborate line to get a willing bedmate for your weekend away from home. But to be positive, I do think you're being straight with me."

She paused and scanned his face. "Last question." Again she hesitated. "Am I right?"

He inched to the edge of the bed toward her chair. Feet on the ground, reaching for her hand on the arm of the chair and looking at her square in the eyes, he said, "Everything I've told you is the truth. If anything can happen beyond Monday, I would be delighted. And if it doesn't, I'm not sure what I'll do."

She grasped his hand. "Pull me out."

Face to face, her tears welled. He removed her glasses and kissed them away.

* * *

Brad wished there was a way he could convince Kate he was genuine and hadn't lied to her. He wasn't playing games, and he was sure she was being up front with him, too.

Previous to this weekend, he had perhaps clung to a forlorn hope that things could be patched up between Jill and him. That might have been why he had accepted that separating would be harmful to James. It needed something like this meeting with Kate, and the immediacy of whatever was happening between them, to shake him out of his apathetic acceptance of Jill's exploits.

Kate was in the bathroom, doing whatever had to be done before they settled down. It had been taken for granted she was spending the night, and both were delighted at that prospect.

She came out of the bathroom, wrapped in the hotel bathrobe and carrying her clothes, which she deposited on the armchair. "You gave me the right answers, Mr. Anderson. I'm bought, paid for, and waiting for you."

Just when the casually tied belt on Kate's robe came undone and the robe opened, his phone rang.

He glanced at the call display. Jill.

Chapter 17
Consolation and Reconciliation?

8:00 p.m., Saturday, October 24th
Treetops Terrace, Kirkland

James could tell something wasn't right. His mother had gone upstairs after supper without clearing off the table. He bet she'd asked Harry to put stuff in the dishwasher and he forgot. For a moment, James thought about putting the dishes in the dishwasher himself, but then he remembered the last, and only time, he did that. He had put plastic stuff in the dishwasher that wasn't supposed to go there, and his father had to call a repair guy. Ever since, he'd been banned from using it, which wasn't a totally bad thing. Despite that, he decided to find Harry and, between them, they could help their mother by cleaning up the kitchen.

Harry wasn't in the basement, so he must be in his room. Probably texting his friends or that girl who had come to the house a couple of times when his mother was out. It was almost as if Harry wasn't interested in his younger brother anymore. He wouldn't play games, saying James wasn't old enough or good enough to play those Xbox games Harry and his friends played. Why wouldn't Harry help him get better at them? And what was going on with his mother? Couldn't Harry tell him that?

At the top of the stairs, James paused. What was that noise coming from his mother's room? Was it his mom's TV or was she crying? He leaned against the door, straining to hear. Definitely his mother. She was sobbing. He should help her. But what could he do?

He hesitated. She didn't like him barging into her room. Harry would know what to do, so he quietly shuffled to his brother's bedroom, where the door was also shut. James heard sounds of Harry's favourite game and knocked on the door.

"Just a minute." The game sounds continued.

James banged on the door, but not too loud his mother would hear. "Come on, Harry. It's me. Something's wrong with Mom." When there was no response, he broke Harry's rule and opened the door.

"Oh no," Harry shouted.

James knew his brother was referring to the game and not to James' sudden presence.

Harry finally got off the chair and came to the door. "Thanks, kid, for ruining my game."

"Something's wrong with Mom."

"Yeah, so what. She was upset at supper. She didn't eat anything and couldn't get away from the table fast enough."

"She didn't even clean up the kitchen. There's pots and pans all over. And dishes. Come listen at the door. Something's wrong. Maybe we should go in and talk to her."

Harry sighed, but he followed James down the hall. Harry knocked on his mother's door. "Mom, are you all right? It's me and James. Can we come in?"

* * *

At the knock on her door, Jill's instinctive response was to control her tears and emotions. The boys shouldn't see her like this. She called out, "Go away. I'll be out in a minute," but a stifled sob broke free in mid-sentence.

"What was that?" Harry's voice came through the door. Behind it, her baby's question, "Can we come in, Mom? Why are you crying?"

Even when distressed and not thinking straight, she couldn't resist her youngest's plea.

"Give me a sec." She got up, straightened the bed, and checked herself in the mirror. It would take her a half hour to get her face anywhere near normal. "What the hell," she said to the image in the bathroom mirror. "They know I've been crying. Let them see signs of damage because of their father."

She opened the door. Harry stood back while James, now almost as tall as her, gave her a bear hug.

"Woah, careful. You're forgetting how big and strong you are."

Harry interrupted. "James was worried when he heard you crying and came to get me. What's wrong, Mom?"

She retreated back into the room and plonked to the queen-sized bed. She leaned against the pillows and fancy cushions and patted the bed on either side of her, inviting her sons to join her. James snuggled beside her, and she put her arm around him.

Harry appeared tense and uncomfortable. "Don't like to see you crying, Mom. James and me, we don't understand. Does it have to do with what we talked about last night?"

James squirmed away from her. "What? When last night? I don't remember talking."

"Oh, it was long after you'd gone to bed, James. Nothing important. Just that I heard from the person I was going out with tonight. Some very nasty things were said to me, and tonight's meeting was cancelled. That really upset me."

"Auntie Chrissie?" James asked.

"I don't think so, James. It was probably that 'A' person. Right, Mom?" Harry asked.

She couldn't help but see the smirk on Harry's face.

James sat up. "What 'A' person?"

She moaned and gripped James' hand. She explained that she and his father hadn't been happy lately and were having difficulties. "That's why I've been going out a lot. But when Dad comes home, we'll all talk about it."

"So, when you and Dad talk about it, you can fix things and everything will be all right?" James stared at her, his mouth quivering.

All she could say was, "We hope so, James. We hope so."

James snugged back against her. She was grateful for his comfort, certain he didn't realize he gave as much as he sought. She exchanged glances with Harry and mouthed "thank you." Though she was annoyed with his attitude, his mention of the "A" person had opened the conversation. He shrugged.

"Okay," she said, "I left a mess in the kitchen. Any volunteers to help me clear away?"

James freed himself from her embrace, saying, "I can clear the table and bring things into the kitchen," and he bounded out of the room to her shouted plea, "Be Careful!"

Before Harry could leave, she put her hand on his arm as a dual token of restraint and affection. "Thanks, Harry. You were very fair when you could have dumped on me again, since you know more than you should. But Aaron and I are finished. That's another reason I was crying. And because your father can't be home tomorrow, which upset me, too. Then again, maybe I need an extra day to get my head straight."

Harry got off the bed. "I'll go check on James. Take your time, Mom. You look a mess. No wonder Arsehole finished with you." He laughed and exited the room.

She waited a few minutes and then went to the top of the stairs. "I'm staying home tonight. Is there a movie we can watch together?"

* * *

James carried the dirty plates and cutlery into the kitchen. Harry loaded the dishwasher and rinsed out the pots and serving dishes. After James put away the placemats and carefully replaced the heirloom pottery bowl exactly in the middle of the round table, he returned to the kitchen and sat on a stool by the island.

After Harry turned off the faucet and the kitchen was quieter, he threw a question at his brother. "Mom and Dad can fix things, can't they, Harry?"

James sensed Harry's delay tactics. The frypan was already dry, but Harry gave it an extra wipe.

"We'll have to wait and see what happens, James. Mom and Dad have to do what's best for all of us."

Chapter 18
Hard Facts and Hard Heart

9:00 p.m., Saturday, October 24th
Phone from Treetops Terrace, Kirkland, to Chrissie in Beaconsfield

By the time Jill got downstairs, Harry and James had cleared away the dishes and turned on the dishwasher. They were trying to agree on a movie, but she sensed no great enthusiasm existed for such a family togetherness time.

She said she wasn't in the mood for a movie and that she had a couple of phone calls to make before bed. "You should go to bed soon, James."

James tried to prolong the time, but his manipulations only got him TV or game time until ten—in his room. Once he'd gone, she checked with Harry that he wasn't headed out or expecting friends.

Harry grinned. "No, Mom. I figured I'd be babysitting James while you were out this evening. But it's not too late. I'll text a couple of girls and see if they want to hook up. No, on second thought, I'll stay home and babysit my poor old mom who's just been dumped!"

She threw a cushion in his direction. "You're grounded."

He laughed. "Got a game to finish, Mom. Glad you can see there is a funny side to your situation." He disappeared from the kitchen.

She understood that making fun of her predicament was Harry's way of avoiding reality, but she was glad his attitude had improved. She wished she could avoid reality, but a knot tightened inside her when she remembered what Aaron had said and done, and the lies and manipulation soared to the forefront.

She needed to talk to someone who understood, someone who could keep quiet about the situation. Chrissie knew about Aaron and would offer a sympathetic ear. But it was Saturday evening, and it would be a miracle if a party girl like Chrissie was home.

Jill turned off the TV, checked the doors were locked, turned off lights, and went to her room for privacy.

* * *

Chrissie had just put down her cell after talking to Georges when it rang again. She didn't have time for long conversations and ignored the call. Georges was picking her up in thirty minutes, and she needed that time for a stiff drink. Somewhere in Pierrefonds, he had said, was a party right up her alley. She was dolled up and had been waiting for his call since eight o'clock. The clock showed it was after nine. That Georges! Always late. But at least he had the decency to call to say he was on his way. If the place she remembered was where she had once partied with him, the good times had continued into the wee hours, and she hadn't returned home until after breakfast. Lots of time.

Less than a minute later, the cell buzzed again while she was applying lip gloss. She still hadn't poured a drink. Chrissie glanced at the call display. Jill. What did she want? Maybe another party she and Aaron had found?

She sighed and picked up the phone. "Jill, you stranger. How are you? Where are you on this Saturday night?"

"I'm stuck here at home. Do you have time to talk?" Jill asked.

"Georges is on his way to take me to a party in Pierrefonds. I think you and Aaron were at that last one? Wasn't that the one where you found him with that teenager? How is he, by the way? Are you still seeing him, or has Brad finally put his foot down?"

There was no response from the other end of the line.

"Are you still there, Jill? What's wrong? Are you crying?"

Jill was definitely crying. Her voice was faint and almost hesitant. "He finished with me earlier today. Gone back to screwing around with those young things he enjoys seducing. I thought we had something, Chrissie. I—"

"Oh, Jill. I'm sorry. But I'm not surprised. Aaron doesn't play for keeps, and I hate to say, you're too old to satisfy his kinks."

"I know."

Chrissie heard sobbing and was torn between Jill and Georges. But Georges was about due, since he'd called to say he was on his way, so she didn't feel guilty taking the easy route. "I'm sorry I don't have time to listen and help you right now, Jill." She searched for impossible words of comfort. "At least you have Brad. Take my advice. Stick with him even if he is—what did you call him once?—a cold fish? At least he's still in the picture. My ex took off so fast when he found me playing away."

Jill was still crying. "He knows about Aaron, and I told Brad I was leaving him for Aaron. It was just a matter of when I would go. Now Aaron's dumped me."

"Oh shit. Did you ever screw up. Here's my quick fix. It's all I have time for. Girl, you should do all you can to get back with Brad. Use all your moves and play him like a hot-blooded game fish. As for Aaron, he's a loser. His life is run by his crotch. Likes young girls too much and doesn't even care how young. Remember that other time you walked out on him at Pepe's? Aaron took me home that night because I was too stoned and stupid to know what I was doing. You are well rid of that loser, Jill." She looked out the window. "Whoops. Georges is here. Be happy. Go to work on Brad. Talk to you tomorrow. We can form a strategy to win back a husband. Ciao!"

Chrissie was glad to end that conversation before it scarcely began.

* * *

Jill brushed at the tears streaming down her cheeks. She should have known better than to expect sympathy from Chrissie. They went back a long way. She and Brad had been friends with Chrissie and her ex until they broke up and Chrissie became the party girl. Anything, anywhere, anybody—as long as she had a good time and could keep up with the party crowd.

But she had phoned Chrissie for advice even though what she needed was sympathy and understanding. And she did get advice, without diplomacy or soft soap.

Why was Aaron such a bastard when he was so attractive in every way—if you didn't count straying and his inability to resist the young things?

But Chrissie was wrong about Brad. He really wasn't a cold fish. He was good for her and had been good to her until she got itchy feet—or something. Could she win him back? Sure she could—if she wanted to.

Chrissie was right. They should talk strategy the next day.

Chapter 19
Interruption and Interference

9:30 p.m., Saturday, October 24th
Phone from Treetops Terrace, Kirkland, to Historic Properties Hotel, Halifax

Jill checked on the boys. They'd already raided the fridge. Both were settled in their rooms, James already half asleep. She'd given up on Harry's sleep habits. Sleep came when the tweets and texts stopped and the game was over.

Back in her room, she decided it was as good a time as any to start working on Brad. It was 10:30 p.m. in Halifax. He'd be back at the hotel by now. Maybe they could talk. She could tell him it was all over with Aaron and that she wanted to try again.

When she realized, once again, that she and Aaron were no more, she suppressed a shudder. Time with him and the excitement she had experienced was close to the surface and could easily be rekindled if she was foolish enough to pursue him or allow herself to be trapped in his web of deceit.

She pictured good old dependable Brad, whom she needed more than Aaron at the moment. Besides, other Aarons were out there—if the urge occurred again.

She found her phone and got her husband on speed dial.

* * *

Brad's first instinct was to ignore Jill's call. Kate was leaned back on her elbows, making no effort to cover herself with the robe, one leg bent, and a "come hither" smile adorning her scrubbed face.

"My wife's timing has never been good. Now it's annoying," he said, letting the call go to voice mail. When he joined Kate on the bed, they heard, "Pick up, Brad. This is important. It's James."

Kate edged away from him, covered herself with the robe, and fastened the belt with an emphatic tug, saying, "You'd better talk to her. If you don't, she'll keep interrupting."

"Shit! I'm sorry, Kate. I'll make it brief."

He called Jill, who picked up immediately.

"What is it now, Jill? What's this about James?"

"He knows that we might be splitting up and—"

"What! How does he know? I thought you were going to keep it from him until I got home on Monday. Who told him?"

"Calm down, Brad. It's happened, and now we have to deal with it. Can't you get here tomorrow? Is work so important you can't come home? We need to sort this out."

Kate's hand grasped his free one.

"I have to stay here until Monday. I have a meeting about a contract," he lied as he squeezed Kate's hand. "How much does James know? And how did he find out?"

"Aaron finished with me today. For good. I was upset, and James heard me crying. The boys came into my room to see what was wrong, and I told him you and I weren't happy together. I said we'd talk about it when you got home."

"And you didn't blame Aaron, I bet. What did James say?"

"First, he wanted to know why you weren't coming home until Monday. I can give him your bullshit excuse if you like. Christ, Brad! He's thirteen, going on ten. He thinks you're coming home on a white charger to sweep me off my feet and everything will be back the way it was."

Brad couldn't resist. "Before Aaron."

"I told you he's history. Get over it. James is the issue now. He's confused. Just get back here as quickly as you can and let's sort this out."

"I'll get there when I can," was all he managed to say before Jill disconnected, believing as always, he thought, that she'd had the last word.

* * *

Jill was almost as mad at herself as she was at her husband when she cut him off. "Well, Jill," she muttered, "that was a great start at winning back his affection."

For a moment, she considered calling him back to apologize and to try to mend the latest hole in the marriage bond. Then she realized he was as angry as she was and only time would calm them down.

If only she had someone to talk to. Chrissie had been too abrupt when they'd last spoken. A year ago she could have talked to her mother, but her mother had found out about Aaron and her running around on Brad. The resultant row meant subsequent conversations avoided marriage issues.

She vowed not to call Aaron, and if he called her, she would not succumb to his sweet talk and idle promises.

Her other friends were happily married or peacefully divorced and would have little understanding of, or sympathy for, her situation. Even if they did understand, they wouldn't want to become involved. There was the office, but she wasn't close enough to anyone there to confide in.

Maybe it was all a myth about those confiding and supportive women's groups, posing as book clubs and always available to share mutual or individual problems. Or perhaps she was the unlucky one whose behavior had her labelled as an outcast.

She was getting maudlin. Her problem, and she'd have to solve it. She'd start by calling Brad the next day. She would be all sweetness and light and wouldn't rise to any provocative comments.

She went down to the kitchen and poured herself a glass of wine. At the first sip, she silently toasted to "winning back Brad." Instead of taking the bottle back to the bedroom with her, she placed it back in the fridge. She needed a clear head to begin her resurrection campaign the following day.

Chapter 20
Moral and Immediate

10:40 p.m. AST, Saturday, October 24th
Historic Properties Hotel, Halifax

Kate usually enjoyed speculating on the unheard half of telephone conversations. But all that she got, as she listened to Brad's responses to his wife, was that their youngest son realized all was not well and neither Brad nor his wife was happy with that turn of events. She also heard Brad lie about a Monday business meeting. If they continued past the weekend, was this how it was going to be: lies and deceptions?

After the conversation, Brad sat on the bed beside her. She was lying on the pillows, her arms folded and body tense.

"Sorry about that, Kate. Give me a second, and I'll tell you what that was about."

She got off the bed, walked to the minibar, and found a scotch. Not knowing whether Brad liked scotch, she unscrewed the top and poured it into a glass. "Neat or with water? Sorry, there's no ice."

* * *

"I'll take it neat," Brad said. He drank as though it was a shot. With a pat on the duvet beside him, he invited Kate back to the bed.

"I should have known something would get in the way of our togetherness time." He sighed and combed his fingers through his hair. "Apparently Jill's boyfriend, the one she said she loved and was leaving me for—well, he dumped her today. Can't say I'm surprised. His type preys on women like Jill, and she's stupid enough to think it's for real and forever. Thing is, they're both so fickle they might just get back together sometime, maybe even tomorrow." He laughed. "I'm not holding my breath while that happens."

Kate snuggled closer and linked her arm through his. "Think about what you're saying, lover man. You might be describing us." She tilted her head and kissed him on the cheek.

Brad defended himself. "There's no similarity between me and that—that lounge lizard, Aaron. And you didn't throw yourself at me like she did at him. Did you?" Brad turned and grinned at Kate. "Now, where was I? Oh yes."

Kate lightly punched him on the thigh, which brought him back to the seriousness of his situation.

"I don't know how this changes things, and I won't know until I get home and talk to all three of them. But that's what I know now. And this is how I want it to be with us—everything out in the open."

He felt Kate trying to get closer though that was impossible. She encouraged him by saying, "If I didn't think you were being honest with me, I wouldn't be here. Keep going."

"James must have heard Jill crying after Aaron gave her the 'Dear Jill.' It seems that James was told that Mommy was unhappy because she and I were not getting along, and it would all be sorted out when Daddy got home. James believes when I walk through the door I'll work a miracle."

"And Jill wants you home tomorrow? That was a lie about a Monday meeting, wasn't it?"

"My meeting is Monday afternoon in Montreal," he said. "And yes, it was a lie. Either way, I'll be home by six, and then Jill and I have to make sure the shit doesn't hit the fan in front of the boys. Jesus, Kate. I shouldn't have goten you embroiled in this mess." He switched position so he could embrace her.

"Do you want to go home now?" she asked.

He hoped she wanted a negative response. "Do I? Hell! I need time to cool down and talk to you about this. Even though it seems unfair. But do you want to leave?"

She broke away from him, and for a second he wondered if she was about to dress and head home. Instead she kneeled on the bed in front of him, grasped him by the biceps, and looked directly into his eyes. "We have idealised this weekend as an adventure. We said it was separate from our other lives. And that's what it is. They start again on Monday. And we will deal with our other halves' interference—if they dare do it again—if it happens, when it happens. Until then, Mr. Anderson, I have spent enough of my life arguing in a bed with my ex. I'm here to enjoy you, in this bed in this luxury hotel, as my other persona."

She paused and a grin broke out. "But before we . . . um, retire for the night, I should forestall another interference and check on my daughter. She's probably been trying to get me for hours. I'd forgotten I turned off my phone for an interruption-free dinner. After that, I'm all yours. Immediately. Is that all right, Mr. Loverboy Anderson?"

Kate was working hard to help him escape reality. He did wonder why she wanted to check on her daughter at nearly eleven o'clock at night. But her reality did not spoil the mood she was trying to create.

"Go ahead, if you don't think it's too late. I'll get another scotch from the minibar. Can I get you anything?"

While she scrambled in her purse, she asked for a wine.

* * *

Before Kate could phone Jenny, Brad said he had something to tell her. He was talking to her back since she had turned and was searching the depths of her purse for her cell. She stopped and faced him.

"I know you have to call your daughter, but no matter what comes from this call, or any other from our families, you need to know that what's happening between us is magic. There's some witchcraft trying to ruin it, but it's not going to be ruined."

She placed her purse on the bed and stepped toward Brad.

"Wait. I haven't finished," he said, holding up his hand, palm toward her in the "stop" position. "This is one of the nicest things that's ever happened to me, and I hope it doesn't end on Monday. If it does, we will have done our best to make it last longer. Now, how about you make the call, and then we can get back to the magic."

She flung herself at him. "You have no idea what all this means to me, Brad. I promise I'll make this quick, and then you can wave that magic wand—or something."

Jenny answered before Kate had a chance to untangle herself from her lover.

Chapter 21
Check Up and Check Out

11:00 p.m., Saturday, October 24th
Phone from Historic Properties Hotel, Halifax, to Jenny's Cellular

"Where have you been, Mom? I've been trying to get you for ages." Jenny had been frantic when she couldn't reach her mother.

"Sorry!" her mother responded. "I turned my phone off. And then it needed charging. I should have checked my texts earlier, but I was having such a lovely evening."

"Oh, tell me more." Her curiosity made her forget her own distress.

"I'll tell you all about it when I see you. What's got you so worked up you needed to talk to me?" her mother asked.

Jenny sensed her mother was trying to keep her away from questions she didn't want to answer over the phone, and she didn't like it when her mother added, "Can you make it quick, sweetheart? I have people I need to say goodnight to."

She ignored her mother and rambled on anyway. "Okay, well first, I'm sleeping over at Cheryl's place. You remember where that is? That apartment off Larry Uteck? Can you pick me up here tomorrow morning about eleven?"

"No problem, Jen. Text me the address. But why are you there?"

Jenny figured her mother was wondering whether the sexual exploits of her father and his hot-to-trot Suzie had driven her away.

"Long story short, Suzie and me had a great afternoon shopping. We got the jeans and a top—oh, and some makeup. But when we got back to Dad's, well . . . it got crazy cos Suzie didn't like that you'd been there when she wasn't. That started the fight. I went to my room when Suzie got really vicious and foulmouthed after Dad told her what you'd come to talk about. She blamed me for complaining about . . . well, you know. She blamed Dad for even letting you in and then for listening to your complaints. Dad pulled her away when she came banging on my door, blaming me for starting it all by telling—"

"She didn't hurt you, did she?"

Jenny heard the concern in her mother's question.

"No, Mom. I had the door locked. She ranted and swore at Dad and then stormed out of the apartment, yelling that she never wanted to see him again. Dad ran after her but couldn't catch up before she took the elevator down to the garage. When he got down there, he said that she almost ran him over. Oh, Mom, it was awful!"

"You're right. Horrid! That's why you went to Cheryl's?"

She got the drift that her mom wanted to know more, but did she want to hear the long version? She had said she was in a hurry. She continued anyway. "When Dad came back up and Suzie obviously wasn't going to answer her phone or respond to texts, we straightened up the apartment, and then Dad said he'd have to go find her. The state she was in, he was afraid what she night do. He asked if I wanted to go with him. Duhhh! Dumb question. I thought it was a dumb idea to even look for her, but you know Dad. Anyway, he said I could stay at his place but maybe it would be better if—"

Jenny smiled when the motherly guilt she'd triggered brought forth another interruption.

"Oh, I'm sorry, Jen. I should have been there for you. How did you get to Cheryl's?"

Despite the concern in her mother's voice, Jenny sensed she wanted to end the conversation. What was going on? First, her mother couldn't be found, and now, with all the drama, she wanted graphic details, and then she didn't.

She had to convince her mother she was safe and sound. "While I was waiting for you to reply, I texted Cheryl to tell her about my day. She already knew all about Suzie—well, not about today's explosion, but the other stuff. She asked her mom if I could come for a sleepover. By then it was almost eight, so she came and picked me up in her mom's car. You knew she'd got her license? I told you a while ago."

"Yes, I remember that."

Jenny knew her mother was lying. She didn't remember.

"As long as you're safe and you don't want me to come and get you, I'll go and say goodnight to my guest. Are you sure you're okay?"

This was so unlike her talkative mom, ever willing to listen. Something was going on. Jenny would find out the next day. Neither could keep a secret. That was something she and her mom had in common.

"Have you anything to tell me?" Jenny asked. "Who's the guest?"

"Not right now, sweetie, but call me on the cell if you need me. The landline isn't reliable these days."

Whoops! Jenny thought. *There's a pork pie. A great big fib if ever I heard one.*

"Right, Mom. But if something's going on, I'll find out tomorrow. Eleven sharp, okay? Oh, and Mom, I know you don't care, but I think Dad and Suzie are history. And it has nothing to do with what just happened. She was asking me this afternoon if she was too young for him. Must have had a premonition, eh? Okay, 'night, Mom. See you tomorrow." She couldn't resist teasing. "Where are you, by the way?"

"Tell you all about it in the morning, Sherlock with the suspicious mind."

"Bye, Mom." She grinned when she turned to Cheryl to tell her of her suspicions. It promised to be a long night of gossiping. But she wished she knew more.

* * *

Brad raised his eyebrows at Kate when she set down her phone. "Problems?"

She quickly processed Suzie's actions and the possible repercussions. "I don't think so. Jenny's at a friend's place because her dad and his girlfriend had a row and she walked out."

"Jenny's walked out? Should you go find her?"

Kate laughed. "No, my daughter is safe and sound at a friend's. Suzie's the one who left, but I think Mike is well rid of her. Apparently, he's headed out to see if he can find her. Can't imagine why. But it's his life."

"Interesting," Brad said. "I've found you and you've found me. In the twenty-four hours we've known one another, both our former loved ones have been dumped. The gods are favouring us. Or are they?"

"That might be a good question." But she wondered whether Mike and Jill might want to slink back to try to win the affections of her and Brad. Not Mike, she figured. She didn't know enough about Jill to make a guess. She hoped Jill the Jilted wouldn't come back to Brad, but if she did, would he succumb?

I am not going there tonight was her resolution. She slipped out of the robe and joined Brad in their hideaway from life, beneath the covers.

* * *

Jenny was still awake long after she and Cheryl had let their imaginations work overtime, speculating where, with whom, and why her mother had been avoiding her. Some of their speculations were too funny and ridiculous. She still wasn't sure that her mother had been anywhere or had done anything she needed to keep hidden.

The last thought, before sleep finally took over, was that she would have an interesting conversation with her mom later in the morning.

Chapter 22
Drunk and Indecisive

2:00 a.m., Sunday, October 25th
Highway Condominiums, Bedford

Mike managed to support Suzie with one hand while extracting his wallet to pay the taxi driver with the other. She was no help getting the doors open and was totally incapable of pressing the right buttons to unlock them. But at least he had convinced her to come home and was pleased with himself for that. His thoughts continued while he opened the door, dragged her into the fortunately empty elevator, and then into the apartment. As gently as possible, he deposited her on the bed.

Almost immediately, she rose and staggered to the bathroom. He followed and closed the door to offer privacy even though her drunken state wouldn't recognize such. The closed door couldn't muffle sounds of retching.

While waiting to see if she could emerge unaided, he thought over his rescue act. Predictably, he'd found her in one of their favourite downtown hangouts, getting lucky on only the third bar he'd checked. She had tried to ignore him, pretending to socialize with the guy who'd bought her what was clearly not her first drink. When the stranger objected to Mike conversing with her, he'd surveyed the size, disposition, and lack of a support group. Reassured by these, he told buddy that Suzie was his wife, which to his surprise, she did not deny. He said he was taking her home and was prepared to meet buddy outside if necessary. He then offered to buy buddy a drink before he and Suzie left, which buddy accepted, obviously cutting his losses.

Mike had taken Suzie by the elbow and suggested they find somewhere to talk. Again, there was no resistance. They walked to a quieter bar with Suzie accepting his arm around her waist. Once seated in a relatively quiet corner of the music-free sports bar, he was surprised when she apologized. Though her speech was slurred, she was oddly coherent.

"I'm shorry, Shweedie. Bud I hade it when tha' woman inderferes wid us. She don't want you. She juss wans to condrol you shtill. You gotta learn to shay no when dat bitch wans to see you to talk aboud someting."

Mike sipped his drink and nodded. He defended his afternoon meeting by saying that Kate hadn't told him why they had to talk, only that it was important.

The peacemaking took three rounds of drinks and consumption of a lot of humble pie.

When they finally left the bar, they seemed to walk forever until Suzie eventually remembered the parking garage where she'd parked her car. The way things were going, neither of them was driving anywhere, and he called for a cab.

He understood why Suzie had gotten so wasted when she said she'd connected with an old friend. Whatever he'd sold her had messed her up.

* * *

Suzie came out of the bathroom, still unsteady, grasping whatever furniture would help her get to the chair in the corner of the bedroom. If she reclined on the bed, the room would go round and round, and she'd be nauseous again.

She should never have taken those pills. She hadn't even asked what they were. Bubba told her they'd level her out if she was uptight, which anyone could see she was, especially when someone tried to chat her up. That good-looking dude, who had been persistent and bought her two martinis, would have taken her home. Or somewhere. She was feeling good and relaxed until Mike found her. She should have known he'd come looking, possessive as he was. Then again, if she hadn't wanted to be found, she could have gone to a bar they'd never been to.

Martini Dude had backed down when Mike reclaimed her for the price of a beer. Was that all she was worth? A beer? Pretty funny, actually.

She didn't remember much more. That was about when she started to feel out of it. Those extra drinks hadn't helped, but Mike wanted to talk and seemed happy to buy more. Wasn't it enough that she'd said she was sorry? She wasn't sure he'd understood how Kate's interference had made her feel.

She wished she had stuck with Martini Dude. She was almost sure she didn't want to be with Mike any longer. She'd had an opportunity to send him away but didn't. Too messed up by drinks and pills. And so much going on in her head. Still was.

And then, in a flash, she was back at Mike's. Didn't have a car to get to her place. She only went there to get clothes and stuff. Hadn't slept there in weeks. He'd been on at her to get rid of it, move in permanently with him. Maybe she should.

Or should she move back by herself for a trial period? What would Mr. Possessive say about that? She corrected herself: Old Mr. Possessive. Well, she wasn't his. He didn't own her.

Old Mike or Martini Dude? Who was the right one? It could have been Martini Dude. But the next day? She wished she knew.

She couldn't think straight. "Can we talk tomorrow?" she mumbled at Mike. "I'm going to sleep in this chair."

* * *

Mike thought he'd said all the right things, but Suzie wasn't listening. She was out of it. The last couple of things she had said made no sense. Something about going to her apartment in Fairview. And then she was gabbling about choosing a Martini.

When he looked in the hall cupboard for an extra blanket, he saw that Jenny's door was open, but she wasn't there. He turned on the light and saw a note on the pillow.

He heard a noise from the other bedroom, so he grabbed a blanket and went back to see if Suzie was all right. She must have slipped off the chair when she tried to remove her leggings. They were around her ankles, and she sat on the floor.

Mike helped her out of her clothes. She didn't object and was too drunk to think he might have ulterior motives for removing her clothing. He retrieved one of his T-shirts, and she slipped it over her head. They manoeuvered her back into the chair. Mike took her pillow from the bed, found the button that reclined the chair, and covered her with the blanket.

When he leaned down to kiss her, she mumbled, "Was dat?"

"It's a note from Jenny. She went to a girlfriend's. Said if I found you that we'd need time alone to sort things out."

"Wha? She needs her mommy? Not a big shister like me. I can't be mommy to a shixtee year old." Suzie's head sank into the pillow where he should have let it rest until morning. Instead, he continued to seek answers.

"What are you saying, Suzie? You don't want Jenny here anymore? Or are you saying we're too old for you? You two are good together. If you accept me, she comes as a bonus. It's been good until today, hasn't it?"

From the pillow came a muffled response. "Don't know any more. Wanna sleep . . . talk tomorrow."

Mike kicked off his shoes and collapsed on the bed.

Chapter 23
Sunday Plans and Introductions

8:30 a.m., Sunday, October 25th
Historic Properties Hotel, Halifax

By the time Kate dressed and was looking her best, breakfast had arrived. She was still trying to decide whether she liked room service meals, but this one gave her the chance to fill in Brad on the previous night's news from Jenny. It hadn't been high priority under the covers—or even when the covers were discarded.

"Sorry to spoil the magic, Brad, but I can't remember if I told you what Jenny said. I'm picking her up at eleven. She doesn't know it, but I thought we'd go for lunch after we collect you. You can get to meet her after I've told her all about you."

"All?" Brad's one word question was uttered beneath raised eyebrows.

"That depends." She grinned. "How much I tell her depends on her reaction when I raise the subject of 'My Weekend with Brad'."

"As long as it doesn't come across as 'My Dirty Weekend with Brad from Out of Town'," we'll be okay.

Kate detected anxiety in his tone and assured him it wouldn't be *that* version because that wasn't what was happening. She changed the subject, telling him, "Jenny thinks it might be all over between my ex and his girlfriend. Oh, I guess I told you that already, didn't I? But neither of us are surprised because she's far too young for him. That's another 'Let's wait and see what happens.' We seem to be collecting those, don't we?"

* * *

Brad's attention wandered to count how many "Let's wait and sees" were piling up in Montreal.

Kate brought him back in the direction of the magic by saying she wanted him to check out of the hotel and spend the night at her place—forgetting momentarily it was also Jenny's home, which she mentioned a second later.

He welcomed the suggestion. He still wanted to go along with the idea even after Kate told him he would probably be sleeping on the cot in her sewing room. “It all depends on Jenny’s reactions,” she said.

“I understand that. Poor kid has already been near traumatized by her father’s sexual activity with what’s-her-name. Looks like another ‘Let’s wait and see,’ but I’m not holding my breath on this one.”

He called reception to say he would be checking out and would settle the bill before he left for his meeting. Kate announced she’d get her act together and leave with him. He accepted her offer of a drive to the conference.

“I need to be there at quarter to ten. Can you pick me up afterward, at one? There’s no lunch planned for today.”

* * *

Kate had lunch organized. She had plans to drive somewhere and back with Jenny in the car. It seemed likely that Brad and her daughter would strike up a conversation and get to know one another if they were together in a car. Jenny wasn’t shy, nor was she afraid to ask questions. Perhaps Kate could judge if Brad was being honest with her daughter and discover if she was getting the same information as her—if the conversation got that deep.

“Have you ever been to Peggy’s Cove, Brad? We could drive there and introduce you to the Sou’wester’s lobster rolls. How does that sound?”

“Been there once, but I didn’t eat there.” He turned to raise the blind and pull back the curtain.

“Sunny and warm all day, but windy. Should be great views and spectacular waves if we get the right table.”

She laughed when Brad said, “You can bribe me with a car ride to a scenic spot for lunch. And in return for a lobster sandwich, I promise to be as nice to your daughter as I am to you. Well, nearly as nice. But different. And it’ll be just like home, sleeping alone in an uncomfortable bed.”

Pushing herself away from the table, she walked to the other side and hugged Brad from behind. Kissing his neck, she wondered whether Jenny would understand if she and Brad stayed in the hotel for another night.

She dismissed the idea before it took flight. Eight oh two three. Next time she had to pick a four-digit code or password, that’s what she’d use: 8023. It had been memorable. She wished there was time to *commemorate* their stay one more time, but sometimes reality took precedence over magic.

Chapter 24
Crisis and Crying

8:45 a.m., Sunday, October 25th
From Treetops Terrace, Kirkland,
To Halifax Convention Centre

Brad, making small talk with other delegates, was about to sit at the table. He was one of the "experts" taking part in a roundtable discussion on alternate energy solutions when his phone vibrated. He silently cursed he hadn't turned it off. He reached into his shirt pocket to retrieve it and automatically checked the sender's number.

Jill. As usual, her timing was impeccable.

He excused himself and, while retreating to a quiet corner, snapped into the phone, "What is it now, Jill?"

To his surprise, James' voice responded. "It's me, Dad, not Mom."

"Sorry, James. I'm just about to go into a meeting. What's wrong?"

"When are you coming home? It's terrible here. Mom can't stop crying, and Harry is either in his room with the door locked or talking to Mom. And he won't tell me anything except that everything will be sorted out when you get home."

Brad sensed his son was close to tears. The father in him was torn. Where was Jill in all this? What could he say? He had to be careful because he didn't know exactly what Jill and Harry had told his younger son, but he had to try to comfort him.

"Harry's right, James. When I get home tomorrow, we will sit down and decide what's best. I'm sorry I'm not there now, but go talk to your mom. If she sees that you're upset, she'll take care of you and stop feeling sorry for herself."

As soon as that final phrase came out of his mouth, he knew he had opened another can of worms. But fortunately, James seemed immune and put the onus back on Brad with the question, "Why can't you come home today like you were going to? Do you have to stay away tonight?"

"I'll see if I can change things, but I may not be able to. Have you had breakfast yet? Maybe you should talk to Mom. Tell her you've talked to me and that I'll phone her later today. She'll be an old grump if you wake her up on a Sunday, but I bet she has to go to work. Tell her I promised we'll talk when I get home. Can you remember all that? They're waiting for me at the meeting, so I have to go."

"I'll go wake her and tell her you might be home today. That'll stop her crying."

The phone went dead.

Brad visualized James crashing into Jill's room.

"Well, Brad, you handled that one well," he mumbled.

* * *

James had sneaked into his mother's room earlier to take her phone to call his father. He entered her room again, but this time there was no subterfuge other than carefully replacing the phone on the bedside table. James' purpose was to wake her.

"Mom, please wake up. Dad says to tell you that I talked to him and that we'd sort things out when he got home, and that might be today." He couldn't get the information out quickly enough.

His mother rubbed her eyes. "Slow down." She got out of bed. "Be back in a sec."

He thought she took far too long in the bathroom, but she looked much better when she emerged.

She hopped back into bed. "Come here," she said, patting the space beside her. "Tell me again what your father said."

More slowly, James gave her the gist, flavoured by his interpretation of his dad's news.

"Is that it? Did you get things straight?"

"Yeah, I did."

"I'll call him to make sure he comes home today."

"You can't. His meeting has already started. He said he'd call you later."

"Are you sure that's everything?"

"Yeah. But he said that if I woke you up you would make me breakfast and that you'd be glad I woke you cos you maybe had to work this afternoon and looking after me would make you stop crying."

She reached over to hug him. Her tears fell on his shoulder, but he struggled free. Motherly hugs to thirteen-year-olds weren't always cool.

* * *

For the next two hours Brad focused his attention on the discussion and need to promote his belief in alternate energy. He was one of the lucky ones who could put other situations, no matter how crucial, on a back burner and bring his skills and knowledge to current issues.

The session wrapped up at 11:30 a.m., when Brad, amidst the handshakes and platitudes, found himself face to face with the head of his company's Atlantic division, based in Halifax.

Reluctantly, he turned down the lunch invitation, pleading a previous lunch date with friends. But Joe Purdy would not be deterred. He insisted they find a quiet spot so Brad could consider a proposition he wanted to put to him.

Brad put his personal crisis on hold. An interesting hour later he found himself free to face non-work issues. Should he get back to Treetops Terrace? It would make James happy if he did. Jill, too. Harry? Brad didn't know where he stood with his moody and intense older son. Harry might think that, if there was a crisis, his father should be trying to solve it. From the Kirkland perspective, however, Brad should be there.

But he wanted to stay in Halifax. He was able to get into denial whenever he was with Kate.

He decided he'd check flights for the evening. If they were all booked, he could blame the airlines for the extra day away. Not that Jill would ever swallow that excuse.

After having been passed from one agent and airline to another, he was told there was one seat available on the 8:55 p.m. flight. Did he want it? Brad asked the agent to hold.

Decision time. Or was it? He wanted to talk to Kate about it but couldn't.

Stall time again. "I'd like to book that seat. But I'm also booked on tomorrow morning's flight with you. Don't cancel that one. My situation is flexible, but I'll be using one of them."

He gave the necessary booking details and asked for the paperwork to be faxed immediately to the Conference Centre and dispatched to his I-phone. Minutes later, he received the email with flight particulars on his phone.

It was too close to one o'clock to try Jill. Besides, he had to discuss recent developments with Kate before contacting home.

He found his way to the front steps. From a no-parking spot across the street, Kate tooted her horn, exited the car, and ran across the street to greet him.

The shadowy figure in the backseat would be Kate's daughter. Brad hoped he'd be able to talk confidentially with Kate. What would her daughter think of the man her mother had just met who had to fly back early to his wife and kids?

He prayed it wouldn't come across like that.

Chapter 25
Daughter and Dating

11:00 a.m., Sunday, October 25th
Basinview Vistas, Halifax

When Kate pulled up to Cheryl's complex, Jenny and Cheryl were sitting on the front step of the building. Both girls seemed to be enjoying the warmth of the sun.

Kate thanked Cheryl for looking after Jenny, although seconds later she wondered why she had thanked another teen. Both girls laughed, which brought Cheryl's mother, Sylvia, to the door. Kate chatted with Sylvia while the girls enjoyed a giggly conversation, the secrets of which were kept from their mothers.

After the hugged goodbyes and Cheryl's throw-away line to Jenny, "Let me know if either of us was anywhere near close," Kate drove toward the highway.

"Do you fancy a coffee while we talk?"

"Oh yes, please, especially if you're going to share your secrets."

Kate resisted the temptation to take the bait from her daughter though she wondered what her daughter was fishing for. Or did she already know something?

She had wanted to pick the time and place to confide in Jenny, but their favourite coffee shop was close by, so she pulled in there instead. Luckily, there was a parking spot.

They found an empty table. "Don't order too much, Jen. We're going to lunch soon."

To Kate's surprise, Jenny took the initiative in the conversation. "Right, Mom. What's the occasion? Where are we going for lunch? Something's going on, and you know I'll drag it out of you. So, do tell."

Kate's initial thought was the conversation would be an easy one, but she stopped herself from speaking about the topic. Instead she tried to change the subject and take control of the conversation like a mother should. "Anything new from your father? Are you sure he and Suzie are through?"

"Nothing new, and we'll have to wait and see if Dad and Suzie want to work things out. But . . . nice try, Mom. I shared my news when you called last night. Your turn."

Kate sighed. It was time. "If you insist, detective." Then she set some rules. "I'm going to be honest in what I tell you, so I will answer most questions unless they are too personal and none of your business. In return, no judging until you have all the information I want to give you. Agreed?"

Jenny stared with her mouth open from across the table. "This sounds serious, Mom. Please tell me you haven't got some fatal disease."

Kate laughed. "No, sweetie, I am well and happy. Why I'm happy is the mystery you've been guessing at."

"Cheryl said you must have gotten a boyfriend. I told her that you don't do that—go out looking for men. Are you telling me Cheryl is right?"

Kate feigned indignation. "Did you two spend all night speculating on your mother's dating and such? Shame on you, Jenny Newman!"

She was surprised when Jenny didn't try to lie but instead said, "You'd be surprised at the things we had you doing. And all the people we had you with in our conversation between midnight and two in the morning. It got to be ridiculous, but funny."

"Do tell," Kate pleaded.

"Some other time, Mom. You were getting serious just now. What exactly do you want to tell me?"

Kate swallowed and then jumped in at her daughter's invitation. "You remember I went out to dinner on Friday evening with some women from work?"

"Course I do! Was it good? No, sorry, don't answer that. Go on with your story."

"It was fun. We finished up at Richardson's. Do you know it?" she asked though she should just tell the tale.

"Sneaked in there a couple of times. It's for younger people, not for you, Mom."

"Thanks, Jenny." She sighed. "I realized that as soon as I stepped through the door. I wasn't planning on staying long though some of the others wanted to. Funny part is that I met someone even though I wasn't looking."

Her words hadn't come out the way she'd wanted, and she tried to get her story back on course. "I'm sorry, Jenny. This isn't easy. You'll have to be patient."

Her daughter reached across the table to touch her arm.

Kat smiled. "It's the fault of those new shoes you helped me choose. My feet were hurting, and I found a seat next to this man who was looking as out of place as I was. Like you say, 'long story short,' we got on well, and I've been seeing quite a lot of him yesterday and this morning, and we're going to lunch with him, and he's spending the night at home with us. . . ." She let out a long sigh of relief.

Her daughter waited for more, so she added, "His name is Brad, and he's a couple of years older than me. I know you have questions. What else do you want to know?"

* * *

Jenny was astounded at her mother's story. Suddenly, she felt grown up with her mother sharing information. As far as Jenny knew, her mother hadn't dated since she kicked her dad out, and that was nearly three years ago. In a way, she was relieved her mom had met someone. She was attractive and deserved to have a decent man in her life. She reassured her by saying, "I thought you'd never date again. I always wondered if you were waiting for Dad to reform, but even I know that's not going to happen. I'm so happy that you've met someone. Where does he live? What does he do? And why is he staying overnight?"

Her excitement for her mom and her own happiness diminished when her mother said, "This is where it gets complicated. He's from Montreal, and he's in Halifax for a conference until tomorrow. But this isn't just a weekend fling. If it was, I'd be keeping that a secret from you."

"Oh, so are you planning to visit him in Montreal? Shopping, Mom! Shopping! Can I come?" This was getting better with every revelation.

"Slow down, Jenny. Brad and I are being cautious until things sort themselves out."

"What things, Mom? What's to sort out?" And then the coin dropped. "He's married, isn't he? Mom, you're dating a married man?" She snatched her hand away from her mother.

The seriousness and intensity of their conversation was drawing them to the attention of other clients, which was embarrassing. "Let's get out of here," Jenny said.

Her mother glanced around the room. "Let's go to the car, and I'll explain some more. It's not what it appears. He's a lovely man, Jenny. You'll like him."

* * *

The short walk to the car gave Kate a few minutes to think. Once in the car, she expected Jenny to be more critical of her choice and prospects for a future with Brad. Instead her daughter asked, "Do you love him, Mom?"

Kate smiled.

"Is that the smile of a woman in love?"

"I wish I knew, but I think this is the smile of a mother who expected to be putting that question to her daughter sometime in the next couple of years." She gazed out the windshield. "Here's what I know, Jenny. Brad and his wife are still together because they have two boys. They are scared that the thirteen-year-old won't be able to deal with their separation."

"Hold on a minute, Mom. I was thirteen when you kicked Dad out. I survived pretty well, I think."

"You did, Jen. But all kids are different. Listen up, there's more."

"All good, I hope."

"I'll let you decide," Kate said before she continued. "Brad's wife had a boyfriend and expected to continue with him when she and Brad split up, but it looks like that's over. But separation is still up for discussion as soon as Brad gets home. His marriage is over."

"So he says." Jenny was obviously suspicious. "He isn't just giving you a line like the boys at school do in the hopes . . ." Her voice trailed off, obviously realizing where the completion of that statement would take them.

Kate realized the implication, too. "I'll tell you this much, but beyond that it's too personal. There's a world of difference between sixteen-year-olds chased by oversexed macho jocks in high school and forty-year-old experienced mothers getting involved with their contemporaries."

Jenny was about to say something when Kate changed direction.

"When I decided we needed to have this conversation, I vowed that it would not turn into a parent/daughter lecture. And it won't. Friday night at his hotel was impulse and an escape for both of us. Last night could not have happened if we hadn't explained our situations and accepted each other's. Having him here to meet you and to spend the night should tell you . . ." She couldn't complete the sentence. Sharing confidentialities and explanations with her daughter, who'd been the anchor in her life, was too intense. She dissolved into tears.

Jenny leaned over and put an arm around her, urging her to dry her tears and drive them home. Kate felt better when her daughter said, "I want to know more about this guy before I meet him. But if you think he's on the level, then so do I. Let's go home. You can tell me more later."

Chapter 26
Friendship and Forgiveness

2:00 p.m., Sunday, October 25th
Phone from Chrissie in Beaconsfield to Treetops Terrace, Kirkland

After a shower, three Tylenol, and a black coffee, Chrissie was almost prepared to face the world. Georges had brought her home from his place, where there had been little sleep. The party happenings had been prolonged. It had been a good night, but she needed to get home to start tasks she'd been avoiding. She also had phone calls to catch up on. She decided to make a couple of those and ease herself gently into the more demanding tasks.

She felt guilty about the abrupt way she'd spoken to the hurting Jill the previous evening. She'd given blunt advice when her friend begged for understanding and sympathy. The two of them went back a long way, and Jill had needed a shoulder to cry on. Chrissie wondered why Jill couldn't be as "bulletproof" as she seemed to be. Why did she want to move from one entanglement into another, when the last thing the man she wanted was permanence?

Maybe she should give her friend more guidance. Jill appeared to be going down the same path as Chrissie had—a lost husband and a forlorn hope for a replacement, with partying to fill the void. Maybe Jill could win Brad back. Chrissie should help her with that.

She pulled her fluffy robe around her, topped up her coffee, and snuggled into the armchair. She picked up her cell and clicked Jill's number.

* * *

Jill snatched the phone two notes into the ring tone. Brad must have turned off his phone for the conference and was returning her call, as he'd promised James. She didn't bother checking the display.

"Brad, thanks—"

“Sounds like you’re ready to take him back, Jill. Or have I got it all wrong? Chrissie here. I need to apologize for last night. You caught me halfway out the door, and I was a little abrupt. Right now I have no plans, except chores that I’ll gladly avoid. So, tell me what’s happening.”

“Chrissie, thought you were Brad. Sorry. I can’t remember how much I told you last night, but Brad told James he’d phone when he finished at the convention. That was about an hour ago, and he must still have his phone turned off. If he calls, I’ll have to cut you off. I need to talk to him. There’s so much happening.”

“That’s fine.”

Jill gave details of Aaron’s abrupt breaking up with her, elaborating on her discovery that he was shacked up with a teenage bedmate yet again. She worked herself into an emotional state, where logic and planning had no place. Chrissie, for once, was a patient listener and asked questions that reeked of sympathy.

Chrissie interrupted Jill’s story again. “Can I tell you what I think, Jill? I think he is history and not the history you want to recall with any longing to relive it. He was using you, girl. You were some mature and seasoned diversion—a change from the barely ripe girls he seems to favour. From my own experience, I know he has some attributes that attract and make you wonder if this can go on and on. But it won’t. He’s toast, Jill. Forget him.”

Jill still didn’t want to agree. “But, Chrissie, if that’s what he is, why do I—”

Chrissie cut off her question, insisting, “Don’t keep going there! Move on! Get to hate the man. Think how he led you on, helped break up your marriage, screwed around on you, and dropped you. Probably as soon as some little chickie used the phone number he left on her cell.”

Jill wiped her eyes. “I know you’re right, Chrissie. But it hurts when I think of him and—and . . . give me a minute.”

But Chrissie continued. “Think about this instead, Jill. Moving on can also mean moving back. Tell me what’s happening with Brad and whether you want him back or not. Is that worth working on?”

Jill sniffled and explained that Brad had known about Aaron and that the plan had been for Jill and Aaron to move in together as soon as James was old enough to deal with a separation. “Now it seems that Brad wants to break things up as soon as he gets home. That’s the call I’m waiting for. Brad’s postponed his return until tomorrow because of work, and when he gets home, we’re supposed to talk about this.”

“Now hold on there, Jill. Let me see if I’ve got this straight because I smell a rat, and its name might be Brad. He thinks you still want Aaron, correct?”

"Yes, but not any longer! He knows all about Aaron, and he knows he's dumped me. But where are you going with this?"

"Until last evening he did think that if you separated you would have somebody to go to, right? He didn't know about you and Aaron breaking up before he went away?"

Jill grunted in agreement.

"Meanwhile," Chrissie said, "he phones you from a weekend conference to say that you should discuss separating with the boys as soon as he gets back. But he has to stay an extra day instead of coming home on time to sort out this crucial stuff. And you're not smelling the same rat that I am? Think about it. It stinks!"

Jill's didn't know what to say. Her head spun in a million different directions. "Oh, Chrissie, you think Brad has somebody there with him and that's why he wants to stay the extra night? Is it someone he sees whenever he goes to the office there, do you think? Or someone he takes away with him? Oh shit, Chrissie! Why didn't I see this? And to think how guilty I once felt about seeing Aaron and lying about it."

"Calm down. This is just my speculation, and you know me, always thinking the worst of any man. The extra night and wanting to sort out the separation may just be a coincidence. If it is, do you want to work on winning Brad back, or is he a lost cause? Move back, or move on?"

"I can always tell when Brad's lying. When he gets home, I'll have to talk to him before we talk to the boys. I'll find out the truth. If there's no one else, I'll see how he feels about trying to reconcile. I suspect that Harry might also have told him that Aaron's no longer in the picture. Oh, Chrissie, I did love Brad, but in a different way to Aaron, and—"

"I told you not to go back there, Jill. Move on!"

"But what do I do if Brad does have someone else and doesn't even want to try getting back to the way things were before Aaron?" Jill asked.

"I'm banning that name, Jill! I swear to God that if you say it once more I'm cutting you off."

"Sorry. But what do I do, Chrissie? What if Brad has someone? What's going to happen to James and me?" Jill was disturbed by Chrissie's interpretation—or was it just speculation? She didn't know, but she saw it as a "what-if."

Her friend seemed to know what she was thinking.

"Don't start with the 'what-ifs,' Jill. Not until after you've talked to Brad, whenever that may be. It's 'let's wait and see' time for now. 'What-if' time comes when you have more facts. Agreed?"

"Yes, I guess you're right. But I wish Brad would phone so we could begin to sort things out."

"He will," Chrissie said. "And if he does have someone, he will be keen to talk about separating from you. I know. I've been there. And when the dust settled, I was left with just the T-shirt."

There was silence on the other end until Chrissie added, "Just kidding!"

"Yeah, right," Jill said, her voice almost a whisper. "I would take him back, Chrissie. I think we could work it out if we could forgive and forget. That would be the best solution for all of us, including the boys. What do you think?"

Jill heard Chrissie's deep breath. "That solution is too perfect. There's a lot of shit going to hit the fan before this is all sorted. Best prepare yourself for it—and for the time it will take. There's hurt and adjustments. There's changes and blame to dish out. All you can do is take one step at a time. First step is that call from Brad."

"You do tell it like it is, Chrissie. And I phoned you last night looking for sympathy. Thanks for this, whatever it is."

"I phoned to offer a shoulder, advice, and support. I also refuse to tell lies to my girlfriends, so here's a final piece of truth. If things go bad and you have to get out, you can always come to me and we can talk things over. I promise. I know you'll want someone to talk to after Brad phones and after—well, after everything. Call me, girlfriend, anytime. If I'm not there, I'll get back to you. Be strong."

"Thanks. I needed straight talk from someone, and it's so good to know who I can call when there's a situation. Talk to you later. Give you another excuse to avoid those chores." Jill laughed and hung up.

Talking to Chrissie had made her realize how much she needed to hear what Brad had to say. Phone in hand, she checked on the boys, who were watching television in the den. "Either of you hear from your father?"

* * *

Chrissie felt sorry for Jill and the situation that would bring more crises. She was surprised she felt good about her conversation with her friend. Her own lifestyle had become self-centred, and she couldn't remember the last time she had offered help and support to anyone with the sincerity she had experienced.

Had she really offered Jill a place in her home if she needed it? What was she thinking? That would cramp her style if it ever happened, which it easily could.

She considered herself a woman of the world, at least in the lost-and-aimless-so-let's-play-around world she inhabited. If she had money to spare, she would bet Brad had someone else. Not that she could imagine it.

Brad had never seemed the type. In fact, he'd turned her down at a party when, friend of his wife's or not, she let him know she was available.

What a contrast between her past and current behavior. She had sincerely tried to help Jill. Perhaps she, too, was ready to make changes in her life. When she'd occasionally stopped to consider her behaviours, she'd realized her current lifestyle had a best-before date—and that date was fast approaching. If she could remove herself from the party animals she spent too much time with, she could find another way to deal with her loneliness.

If Jill didn't work things out with Brad, they could do the find-a-man dating scene together. This was the new Chrissie. Most of the other phone calls she owed could wait until she decided which of her friends needed this new and understanding Chrissie.

She would place the necessary calls. But not until she found out what Aaron was doing and let him know he had succeeded in eliminating Jill from his life.

Chapter 27
Lunch and Letdown

3:30 p.m., Sunday, October 25th
Returning from Peggy's Cove
to West Condos, Clayton Park, Halifax

The atmosphere during the drive to Peggy's Cove had been easier than Jenny had expected. There was none of the embarrassment and discomfort she had anticipated before she was introduced to Brad. He had insisted she call him by his first name even though her mother had introduced him as Mr. Anderson.

First impressions were positive. He was a good looking man with short hair, who looked great in a suit, which he was obviously used to wearing, despite suits being out of place in the Sou'wester Restaurant. She liked his deep and masculine voice. He could stand to lose about ten pounds, but dressed in more casual wear, he'd appear less like a middle-aged businessman and more like her mother's boyfriend.

Jenny had decided that's what he was—her mother's boyfriend. Not because of what her mom had told her, but by their greeting: the kiss on the steps of the convention centre, the hand-holding on the way to the car, and their relaxed conversation.

Brad had asked all sorts of questions about school, her ambitions, and what she did in her spare time. He was genuinely interested, turning around in the front passenger seat to make eye contact with her.

But what won her over was when he said, "Sorry, Jenny, I'm asking all these questions when you must have a few about your mom and I. I'm not sure what she's told you, but fire away. You're due an explanation from me."

She was confused by the invitation, but he was right. She did have questions but wasn't yet comfortable enough to ask them.

He sensed her discomfort. "I mean it, and I'm sure your mom agrees. Let me answer two questions that you must have. Yes, I am very fond of your mother, but I don't know where we are going after this weekend. And yes, I do have a wife and two sons: Harry, who's about your age and is probably going to Dalhousie next year, and James, who is thirteen. My wife and I are going to sort out the details of our separation when I get home. We've stayed together this last year or so because of the boys. Really, I guess, because we didn't think James could deal with us splitting up."

She was relaxed in his company but had blurted, "And what if your wife won't agree to a separation? And if she does, how long will that take? Where does that leave my mom?"

"Jill, my wife, told me she's in love with her boyfriend, who she's been seeing for more than six months. Now it looks like that's over. But we'd already agreed that our marriage is a sham. The boys are just finding out about that. There's a lot to sort out, I know."

She had no response.

"How long will it take? I hope we can agree to separate after we talk this week. Details will take time, and so will divorce proceedings."

Another silence that Brad seemed to think he had to break. "And your mom? She doesn't deserve this mess. But I promise I'll let her know everything that happens after I get home. I want to continue to see her, but only if she wants to. How, when, where, and why depends on me getting unmarried."

Jenny saw her mom's right hand reach over to rest on Brad's thigh.

Her mom glanced at her through the rear view mirror. "I told you that, Jenny. We'd agreed to be honest with one another, and what happens depends on events in Montreal."

Her mother looked from Brad and then back in the mirror. "I'm having a wonderful surprise weekend. I didn't think anything like this would ever happen because I've been avoiding all opportunities. I'd love this to go on, but it's a wait-and-see-what-happens situation."

"Any more questions, Jenny?" Brad asked.

"No, you got the important ones." She was again feeling comfortable until a thought occurred. "Oh, one more. Mom, does Dad know what's going on?"

Her mother replied, "No, and I don't plan to say anything. Last time we talked we nearly came to blows. I'd like to keep it a secret for now, Jen. Agreed?"

"That's good, Mom. He's got enough to deal with right now." Jenny hoped she didn't blab next time she saw him.

The change of scenery, the stunted trees and erratic rocks sticking out on either side of the road, and the grey ocean to their left, announced their approach to the lunch venue. Conversation switched to small talk, with both her and her mother giving Brad information gleaned from many previous jaunts to Peggy's Cove.

The three walked from the car park. Jenny felt safe and comfortable scrambling over rocks and down gullies. It was nice to see Brad lending her mother a hand to prevent her from stumbling in the inappropriate footwear she was wearing. Jenny knew the shoes were for Brad, not for traipsing over rocks.

Seated by a window in the restaurant, with an incredible view of the lighthouse and the waves crashing on the rocks, Jenny was amazed to hear Brad had never eaten a lobster roll. In fact, he had never eaten lobster in any form. He resisted their entreaties to order a whole lobster. Jenny and her mother wanted to see how this lobster virgin would deal with the beast. Instead, he ordered a lobster roll, with apple cobbler for dessert.

The mood was light and relaxed. It was, Jenny thought, as if they'd known each other forever. She had been on similar outings with friends and their parents before separations, where the mood had never been casual and stress had been a part of the families' formula.

Drinking their second pot of tea, the conversation veered to Brad's work. After describing what he did, he amazed them with an announcement. "I was going to keep this a secret, but now seems a good time to share."

Jenny noticed her mother's sudden jerk.

"If I want the position, I can take over as head of the company's Atlantic division when the present head retires at the end of May next year. I'd then move to Halifax." He paused and glanced at her mother. "That would be good news, if other things work out, wouldn't it?"

That's when the mood shifted from warm to icy. Her mother said nothing. The situation had changed in a subtle way. And when conversation began again, it was forced, and there were too many gaps. Something had happened with the announcement he had made, and Jenny wasn't sure what it was.

She decided a trip to the washroom was in order.

* * *

Brad had made a mess of his announcement. The mood and timing seemed right for what he'd imagined would be good news. Once the separation was worked out and the legal issues, living arrangements, and custody initiated, the promotion and move to Halifax would be ideal.

The introduction to Kate's daughter had been great. He had feared the worse. What a lovely and mature girl she was. The only sixteen-year-old girls he knew were those who occasionally visited as part of the group that Harry hung around with. Brad's brother described his teenage daughters as creatures running on the momentum created by random mood swings.

He detected no signs of any moods from Jenny unless the sudden urge to find the washroom when he ended his "good news" was a cover. She and her mom had certainly exchanged looks, the interpretation of which could only be known to a mother/daughter duo. And bless the girl; she took her sweet time in the ladies' room, allowing Kate and him to discuss it.

She let him know his announcement should not have been made and was angry he had chosen to tell her that option. "Don't you see I'm having enough difficulty with you getting on that plane back to your wife and kids? I'm trying to accept that there are so many hurdles in the way that this weekend might be all we have. Then you ignore all the difficulties and present this idyllic future. Worse, you announce it in front of Jenny."

"I'm sorry. I'll put it in context when Jenny comes back."

Kate's "Don't bother" had been a loud, clear message.

Brad knew it was best to say nothing. But he had to say something. It couldn't be left like this. Again, he assured her he did not want this to be a one-off weekend. He wanted more. He saw a future with Kate and her daughter. To get there, details had to be managed, and he was good at managing details. His training as an engineer, tying up details and planning, would help.

That's when Kate said, "Shut up, Brad. I don't like this side of you. Put it away. It's all too soon. We'll talk later."

Seeing an opening, he said, "When we do, I have something else to tell you."

She gave no reaction other than a wave.

Jenny must be emerging from the washroom behind him

* * *

Brad picked up the bill and beckoned the server.

Until his announcement, Kate had thought lunch with her "man" and her daughter would be the highlight of the weekend. She had enjoyed hers and Brad's time together, but hearing Jenny and Brad talking comfortably was almost as good as abandoning her common sense and inhibitions in room 8023.

She tried not to live in "dreamland," but Brad and Jen seemed to like one another. And Brad had set Jenny free to ask about issues bothering her.

The walk on the rocks, given the shoes she wore, hadn't been the best idea, but Brad had been attentive and supported her those times she'd been unsteady. And the warmth, despite chilly October, was pleasant.

She had learned he was a man who liked his food. The lobster roll, coleslaw, and fries were soon demolished. Both she and Jen had told him the next time he'd get the full deal—a whole lobster.

Perhaps the discussion about "next time" had prompted him to announce the possible move to Halifax. *Big mistake!*

Jenny had been perceptive to take a bathroom break, which gave Kate a chance to tell him the news could have kept. She hadn't needed over-optimistic plans when she would be struggling with the what-ifs after the weekend and the pitfalls ahead.

Must be a male thing, she figured. Men didn't know when to stop talking. They couldn't take a hint and change the subject. Not only that, but a new side of Brad's personality had appeared. Were there other aspects of this man that were not so appealing?

She didn't think the "honeymoon" was over, but could she tolerate the Brad she had seen in the Sou'wester conversation? Had she been foolish enough to believe this new man was perfect? No such creature as a flawless man existed, but flawed or not, she still liked most of what she had seen thus far. Perhaps, too, she was upset over something as minor as him sharing what he thought to be great news.

On the drive back into the city, she let Brad and Jenny monopolize the conversation so they could get to know more about each other. Jenny was interested in hearing about Harry and why he was going to Dalhousie. Kate listened carefully, more aware than ever that she had a lot to learn about a man she had just met. One who had captured her affection.

Back in the condo, it was Brad's turn for a washroom visit. After the door locked, Jenny turned to her. "Oh, Mom, I do like him. I hope things work out."

That's what I hoped she'd say, Kate thought. *But it's still too soon.*

Chapter 28
Reverting to Reality

4:30 p.m., Sunday, October 25th
West Condos, Clayton Park, Halifax

When Brad emerged from the washroom, he noticed Jenny wasn't around. "Has she gone?"

"Yes, homework, she said, but I think she wants to give us time together. Smart girl, my daughter, don't you agree?"

"She's easy to get along with. I'm not used to teenage girls, but she's not like the horror stories I've heard and read about. Their moods and rebelliousness and—"

Kate laughed. "Oh, she has her moments. Rebellions are few, but you haven't seen 'the look' yet."

"What's that?"

"Sooner or later you'll disagree with her. Then you'll get 'the look' that says far more than any argumentative words. Enough of my lovely daughter except to say I'm delighted that you two got along so well."

They settled in nearby chairs. He wanted to be close so they could talk quietly. He engineered a move by saying, "I like what I've seen of your place. Love your taste in artwork and pottery," hoping she'd show him around.

"Here, let me give you the grand tour. All except for Jenny's room since she's supposedly busy. And who knows what state it's in."

When they finished, Brad sat on the sofa and patted the seat beside him. "We need to talk."

She sat next to him, and her head rested on his shoulder when his arm went round her. She provided the opening he'd been looking for when she asked about other things he'd wanted to tell her.

He stiffened. "You're not going to like this bit, Kate."

She sat upright and looked directly at him, ignoring his arm that tried to grasp her back to him.

"We said we'd be honest, so tell me."

"This is taking us back to reality because early this morning before the conference I had James on the phone. He was really upset. His mom keeps crying, Harry has shut himself in his room, and he wants to know why I don't come home today."

Kate moved closer and grasped his hand. "And you've been carrying this around all afternoon? I'm so sorry. You should have told me. All I could think about was you and Jenny getting along so well. Then you scared me with your good news. Now this! What did you tell him?"

"I told him I might not be able to change my plans. I told him to wake his mother to get breakfast and tell her he'd spoken to me and that I'd call her later."

"And did you call her before you met us?"

Brad sensed her practical side emerging.

"No," he replied. "Instead I called to see if there was a seat to Montreal this evening. There is. I now have two tickets in my travel folder—one for tomorrow morning and one for eight o'clock tonight."

He waited for the suddenly quiet Kate to say something. He honestly had no idea how she would react. It wouldn't surprise him if she told him to leave and it would all be over. Was she boiling inside at this—this—what was it? Betrayal? Was she about to explode? Would she see this booking as weakness? Would she think his life was still being run by a loveless wife?

The silence was long, and for the first time in his life, he resisted the temptation to break it with superfluous words.

* * *

Kate's thoughts, as well as her emotions, were all over the place. It would be too easy to vent and spew words she wouldn't say if she was in control. Had she been the sort of person who saw the worst option in any situation, she would have seen his actions as total rejection. She had been through her own separation and all the emotional turmoil that accompanied it. She remembered the illogical decision-making and impetuous behaviours and statements that she later regretted. Had she not experienced those, she would have said an emotional and far-from-fond farewell to Brad. Not "au revoir," but "goodbye forever."

But she had been where he now was, except she had only wanted to say "get lost" to Mike. Plus, she'd had no one to move on with—until now.

Brad was beginning the long, uncertain process of closing one relationship and wondering if he had found a better one that could grow, despite the chaos of divorce negotiations.

Her thinking stopped when Brad's ability to tolerate silence ended. "Kate, there's two things I want to do. The first is that I want to spend more time with you tonight. And I have an airline ticket for that. Second, I want to talk with my wife and kids about changes in our lives. I have a ticket that will get me home before bedtime, to calm the boys down and start discussions with Jill. While the boys are in school tomorrow, Jill and I can maybe come to some sort of agreement."

"And am I to decide which plane you take?" she asked, with the first signs of anger in her voice. "I won't do that!"

"Nor would I ask that of you."

His words weren't much of a speech, but they spoke volumes. Thankfully, he explained further. "I decide, but I want you to understand that I am going back this evening because there is a crisis brewing there and the sooner I get involved, face to face with my family, the more I can control it, or at least, steer it in directions favourable to us."

She broke the next extended silence. "Is that it?"

"No, Kate, it isn't. I'll understand if you call a taxi and send me off to the airport right now. One thing I've been forced to confront this weekend is that I am carrying so much baggage it's weighing my life down. The other thing I've recognized is that meeting you this weekend means I have to lighten that load, so I can be fair to you and get my life back in order."

He paused, seemingly to weigh his words. "You don't need me as I am. I think this weekend's free sample gave us both an appetite for a new life. I'm headed to Montreal on the eight o'clock flight, to start unloading and rearranging the baggage. Once I can see the way clear, I want to come back to see you and we can decide what we have."

She pulled away from him, leaned back into the sofa, and closed her eyes.

* * *

The only sound was music coming faintly from Jenny's room. Brad tapped his feet to the rhythm. Anything to stop him reaching for his shoes, jacket, and luggage and heading out the door for the first and last time. He'd made a decision. Could Kate live with it? Did she see any future for them? Or did she see the tonight flight as him choosing the past over their possible future?

Kate's eyes opened, and she turned. Her hand grasped his. Softly and with restraint that gave him hope, she said, "Mr. Brad Anderson, if I hadn't been through separation and divorce, if I hadn't been to places and made decisions that you're just beginning to experience, I would be angrily booting you out of my house and throwing your belongings after you. Instead, this is what I want you to do."

In the pause that followed, he hoped he still had a possible future with this wonderful, understanding woman who might be giving him a chance.

"You'll find a beer in the fridge. Go get one. You need it and, I think—but I'm still not sure—you deserve it. I will drive you to the airport for seven o'clock to go home and get things straightened out. My head agrees that's what you need to do if there's any hope for us, even while my heart wants you to stay."

As he was about to express appreciation for her understanding, she spoke. "There's more. While you phone your wife, I'll tell my daughter what's happening and talk over a few things with her. I need you to promise you'll call me tomorrow night, any time, to report on—for want of a better word—negotiations."

He wanted to say more than "thank you," but Kate put her fingers to his lips.

"Get your beer and phone your wife before I change a mind that doesn't seem to be thinking too sensibly right now."

Kate got up and disappeared down the hall. Brad heard a knock and Kate's clear voice, "We need to talk, Jen."

Chapter 29
Trigger and Ending

5:00 p.m., Sunday, October 25th
West Condos, Clayton Park, Halifax

"Hold on a sec," Jenny said into her phone when her mother's head poked around the door. "Mom, I'm talking to Dad. Can it wait a minute?"

Her mother had always respected her privacy, but not this time. She entered her bedroom and sat on the corner of the bed farthest away from her. Jenny read her lips as she mouthed, "Sorry, I'll be quiet."

"Sorry, Dad. Mom wants to talk to me. Sounds pretty heavy. Okay if I tell her what you've just told me?"

Jenny recognized the quizzical look on her mother's face. Her mom wanted to know what her father was saying. What a crazy day this was turning into. Teenaged daughters were supposed to put their parents through emotional turmoil. But not in her family, where everything seemed backward.

She could only deal with one parent at a time, and her father wasn't making sense. She needed to tell her mother about him—and now. She hoped the goodbyes she prompted were not too hasty, but her father seemed okay.

Before she had a chance to report on fatherly happenings, her mom said, "Brad and I have come to a decision, and I need to share it with you while he calls home. Do you want to go first or shall I?"

"Please tell me it's not over, Mom."

"No, it's not. The weekend is coming to an early close, that's all. Unless your father is screwing things up again. I thought we were past that. What's he done this time?"

"I'm not sure," she said. "He's realized that Suzie is too young for him, and she thinks he's too old for her, and she doesn't want to settle down. Anyway, he's pretty sure it's over. She went off to friends before he even woke up, and he doesn't know if she'll be back."

"That seems to make sense, which is rare for your father where women are concerned. What else?"

"Mom, you promised you wouldn't dump on Dad to me. You might not want to hear this, but you need to. Count to ten before you say anything, please. Dad says—he thinks the best thing he can do is get back with you."

Using the cold, calculating voice Jenny knew was a thin veneer over anger and turmoil, her mother asked to use her phone. When she handed it over, Jenny hoped her mother wouldn't be too hard on him.

* * *

Mike recognized Jenny's number and assumed she was calling back to apologize for her abrupt ending to their conversation. He was surprised to hear Kate's voice.

He recognized the tone of her measured speech. She and Jenny had talked, she said. She was sorry things weren't working out with Suzie but, in view of the age gap, that was almost inevitable.

He was optimistic. For once, she was being reasonable. Maybe she had considered the message he'd asked Jenny to pass on. She hadn't exploded.

But then his three words "What about us?" turned Kate's measured phrases into anger. The pause that followed was a brief calm before the storm.

"How many times? We're over! There's a piece of paper coming from the courts any day now that will tell you that because you don't seem to want to believe me."

The volume was increasing; the speed, too. Emotion overtook reason when she continued. He didn't want to hear what was coming, but he listened.

"You are history. For our daughter's sake, I keep in touch. Any feelings I had for you are long gone, so how you can even think about us getting back together is ridiculous. I've moved on. I am trying to be an adult, but you won't let me. For goodness sake, Mike, grow up. I have given up trying to save you from yourself. I have someone else to throw my affection and support at."

That's new, he thought. *Who has she has hooked up with?*

Kate had said nothing he hadn't heard before. For a moment, he cast the blame on Suzie. Her walking out again before he had even woken up must have thrown his thinking for a loop. He should have known better than to even think of getting back with his wife.

Her voice tore into him again. "Whatever made you think I'd want you back? I can't change you. You don't want to change. Don't ever have our daughter bring messages to me again. Ever! Have you got it this time? We are through! It is over! We are not getting back together!"

She stopped speaking, and the only sound coming at him was Kate's heavy breathing. His cue to answer.

"I hear you loud and clear. Thought it was worth another try. Don't know what I was thinking."

"Enough, I said. Our daughter has heard all this—well, my end, at any rate, so please tell her you understand, and assure her that we'll never get back together."

* * *

Jenny took the phone from her mother.

"You okay?" she asked her father.

"Bruised and battered."

Joking, as usual, she thought.

"Had to give it one last try, but you heard what she said. Call me in a couple of days. You and I can make some plans—just us, no Mom, no Suzie. Maybe you can tell me all about your Mom's new man."

She rolled her eyes at her mom. "Nothing much to tell. Early days. I just met him today."

Her mother made the signal for "cut this conversation" just when her father asked, "He hasn't seen the Killer Kate that you and I have just heard, then?"

"I gotta go, Dad. Have an assignment due tomorrow, and Mom wants to talk to me. Love you."

Kate's thumbs-up sign accompanied her father's farewells.

"Mom, you are so hard on him. He didn't need that shouting."

"I'm sorry, Jenny, but that's all he understands. And he was such a lovely man when I ignored his flaws and could be in love with him. Been there. Done that. Not doing it again!"

Was that an ominous prediction about her mother and Brad? Her mother wrapped her arms around herself, and they slumped back to the pillows. She listened while her mother explained why Brad would be leaving for Montreal and his family in about half an hour.

"It isn't over, is it, Mom?" Why she needed reassurance that Brad was still in their lives was beyond her comprehension. She'd just met him.

"Honestly, Jen, I don't know. I'm free from your father, and you seem to like Brad, so far. But, as Brad says, he has a lot of baggage to sort and unload. Nothing I can do about that. But whatever Brad tells me from now on, I'll tell you. It's a wait and see situation, Jen."

Jenny knew her mother needed a hug. And no more words.

Chapter 30
Agreement and Disagreeable

5:05 p.m., Sunday, October 25th
Phone from West Condos, Clayton Park, Halifax, to Timbertrail Terrace, Kirkland, Montreal

Brad drank his beer and mulled over what he needed to say to Jill. The situation was similar to the last-minute review he'd thought through before his presentation the previous day. Jill was still top of his speed dial and would be, he guessed, for some time. He hoped she had her phone beside her.

"About time," she said. "I've been waiting all day to talk to you."

"Sorry, I've been busy until just now and had my phone switched off. I forgot to tell James that you wouldn't be able to call me."

"Typical," she said. "So, what's coming first—work or your family? When are we going to see you? You know how upset James is. And Harry is totally uncommunicative, and I feel like shit!"

"And that's what you want me to come home to?" He shouldn't react, but she wasn't making things easy.

"If you didn't go away so much, things like this wouldn't happen. Or maybe they would."

She's probably been spoiling for an argument ever since James told her of my call, he thought. He attempted to launch a dove of peace. "I have news you might like."

Jill's "Do tell!" was a guarded acceptance of the peace offering.

"My plane gets into Montreal at 8:35 this evening, your time. Can you meet me without the boys, so we can lay out some ground rules on the drive home? We should agree on what they need to know."

"I suppose so. But I need to know what exactly we are aiming for. Then and after we get home."

"We need to get our separation out in the open since that's where we're going. Even if we can agree on that, it still opens a whole can of worms. I'm taking Monday off. Can you leave it free? With the boys at school, we can get right down to it. Then we can talk to them in the evening. What do you think?"

“Separation?” Jill said. “Are you sure about that?”

“Just because Aaron may be out of the picture doesn’t change the fact that our marriage ended two years ago when you first went looking.”

“Do you blame me?” She seemed ready to vent again. “Even when you were home, you weren’t . . . weren’t—oh, you didn’t give a shit about me. Now you’re talking about a final separation. Have you got somebody else? Is that why you wanted to stay over an extra night?”

Alarm bells rang with her last question. He dismissed his wife’s speculation with, “I don’t know where that idea comes from, Jill. We have a lot to talk about. See you at the airport. Tell the boys it will be good to see them. Anything I need to know before I talk to you and them?”

“Harry blames me for all this. James doesn’t know anything except that you and I aren’t happy together. Harry is angry at both of us. Is that enough?”

He sighed. She had to turn the screw.

Then she added, “Are you sure there’s nothing else I should know about you?”

He was taken aback by the question. How could she know anything, or even suspect? “I’m an open book,” he replied.

“I hope so, Brad. Because if there’s any smut on your pages when we do separate, I’ll find it.” And with that threat, she ended the call.

The silence was punctuated by Kate’s voice coming from her daughter’s room. Though he shouldn’t listen, he detected anger in her voice and figured she was talking to her ex. She was telling Mike, and coincidently Brad, that her marriage break-up was final.

Someday soon, he wished. Soon.

* * *

Kate was almost asleep, snuggling with her daughter, when she remembered Brad.

“I need to talk to Brad, Jenny. He was telling his wife and boys that he was coming home this evening. I could get to hate that woman, even without having met her.”

Jenny shifted her weight, saying “We can talk some more when you get back from the airport if you want. What time is the flight?”

“Around eight. I’ll be back here easily by nine. We’ll snack, and I’ll fill you in on the latest events and answer any questions. Like I said before, I had visions of talking to you about personal situations in about a couple of years, but it was you in the situation, not me. I’m enjoying confiding in you.”

Her daughter laughed. "Go talk to your boyfriend—or something." She pushed Kate toward the door. "Let me know before you leave. I want to say goodbye to him."

"How about, 'See you next time,' instead of goodbye, just for your mother?"

* * *

Brad wondered what was happening. Conversation in Jenny's room had ceased ten minutes ago. Just when he was about to knock on the door, it opened, and he and Kate came face to face. She threw her arms around his neck and kissed him passionately. Watching them through the open door, Jenny piped up, "Get a room, you two! Some of us have work to do."

Jenny got up and closed the door.

He and Kate walked back into the living room. "Was that your ex you were yelling at earlier?" he asked. "If so, remind me not to get on the wrong side of you. You have a nasty side!"

"Oh, he deserved it. He had the gall to ask Jenny to tell me he was thinking he and I should try again. I was simply straightening him out on that misconception. I'm free."

"Wish I was," he said. "Jill's meeting me at the airport without the boys. I told her I wanted to sort out the separation. We're both taking the day off work tomorrow to talk. That's after we agree what to say to the boys tonight. Apparently, James has me coming to the rescue while Harry has me as the villain, along with his mom."

"Is Jill's boyfriend history, or could he be still in the picture?" Kate asked.

"It would be better for us if he was in the picture." He sighed. "I gather he's loved her and left her."

"That makes two of you." Kate laughed while going to the fridge. She poured herself a white wine and flipped off the top of another beer for Brad.

"Back to reality," he said, taking a sip. "How long to the airport from here?"

"If you want to be there for seven, we need to leave here by six fifteen at the latest."

"I haven't unpacked, so I'm ready. This gives us half an hour. Any suggestions, Ms. Hull?"

"I have, but with a sixteen-year-old daughter who's already discovering aspects of her mother that have so far remained private, I believe our options are limited."

He grinned. "Come sit beside me, and we'll behave like a sedate middle-aged couple. Practice for the future."

In response, Kate hitched up her skirt and straddled him on the sofa, again kissing him passionately. “What do you mean ‘sedate and middle-aged,’ Mr. Anderson?”

Chapter 31
Pursuit and Abandonment

7:15 p.m., Sunday, October 25th
Chrissie's House, Beaconsfield, Montreal

Jill's anger at her husband's telephone-talk of separation had clouded her thinking. It seemed he truly wanted to bring their marriage to a close. And was there somebody else waiting in the wings? Perhaps Chrissie was right. Jill told herself to stay calm so she could decide what was best for her and James. Harry was off to university in less than a year, so she wasn't worried as much about him as she was about James. And what about the house?

Had she sensed something in Brad's voice that hinted final legal separation was not a done deal, that it was up for discussion? She wasn't sure; maybe it was wishful thinking.

As she pulled into Chrissie's driveway, Jill wondered if her run-around friend was the best person to consult about Brad's latest call. She eyed the house Chrissie had kept in the divorce settlement, which reminded her of the expensive lifestyle her friend enjoyed. She must have done all right in the painful process despite her claims to the contrary.

Jill knew no one else she could approach for advice.

She had phoned Chrissie as soon as she had finished talking to Brad. Her friend proposed Jill stop in on the way to the airport, so Jill could bounce thoughts and ideas off her. It had seemed like a good idea then, but she was beginning to have doubts. Brad's flight was on time, and she needed more than a half hour to talk and reach conclusions.

When Chrissie answered the door Jill said, "Thanks for this. I wish I had more time to sort out all that's going around in my head."

Chrissie turned from closing the door and tightly hugged Jill. "Auntie Chris is here to help. Now sit down, and I'll get us something to level you out. Wine would be good if you didn't have that messy approach to the airport to navigate. I swear they're always working on those roads in and out of Dorval."

Chrissie returned from the kitchen with a joint already lit and offered it to Jill. “Just a couple of hits and the situation your head is in won’t seem so chaotic.”

After taking her friend’s advice, Jill slumped back in the armchair. “First problem is I don’t know what I want. Do I want to keep him or not?”

* * *

A half hour was not going to lead to decisive thinking, but at least Jill seemed to be focusing on the prime issue. Chrissie offered encouragement. “If he wants you back, you have to lure him, entice him, show him only your positives. Can you do that, given your recent history? How good an actress are you, Jill?”

“Oh, I can play that role well. I’ve added some moves from my time with Aaron that will help win him back. But is that what I want?”

Chrissie introduced another consideration. “When you talked to Brad earlier, did you ask if he was playing away? If he is, you might have lost control of the situation.”

“Oh, I asked,” Jill replied, “but he didn’t answer. I told him if he was that I would find out.”

“That’s an issue that needs immediate investigation. If he has someone else, then whatever magic you think you can work is likely to fail.” She tried to make Jill look at all possibilities. “Do you want him back?”

“I’m not sure, but I’m used to having him around so I can nag him for the times that he’s not around, even when I’ve taken advantage of those times. He’s been my security blanket, my comfort zone while I went off exploring. He’s Brad. Good old reliable Brad who puts up with my shit.” Jill said her last words with her eyes closed.

“If you were divorced from ‘good old reliable Brad,’ behaviour that you describe as ‘shit’ when you’re married wouldn’t be so wrong. Think on that one,” she said. “I do. Every day and some nights.”

“But then there’s the kids, the house, finances, child support, alimony. It goes on and on, and I wouldn’t know where to start.”

“Don’t worry about those issues now,” she said. “That’s why you hire a lawyer. And do it as soon as you, or Brad, decides on legal separation or”—Chrissie paused for effect—“if he is foolish enough to admit there is someone else. I can give you the name of the lawyer who handled my divorce. Look around you. He did all right for me.”

“Like I told you on the phone, Brad and I are spending tomorrow talking about all this. If he has someone else, I’ll find out. If he hasn’t, maybe I’ll say I regret my actions over the last year and that wasn’t the real me. If he’ll forgive me, we could try again. Oh, Chrissie, this is all so confusing. There's the challenge, danger, and excitement of running around, but some days I want peace, quiet, and a normal family life. But how can I sort my life out if I don't know what I want?"

"You sound as sorted out as it's possible to be with all that's happening. Answers take a long time to find. I know. I've been there," Chrissie said. "I'll deny I ever said this, but as much as I enjoy my single-again life, I wonder whether I should have worked harder to save my marriage."

Jill interrupted the awkward silence that punctuated the confession. "I should go in case traffic is jammed at the circle. Where did you get that smoke? It sure calmed me down."

"I have my sources, and if you need a sympathetic ear or any advice or, God forbid, a bed, Chrissie and her medications are always available."

She felt good when she gave Jill a parting hug at the door. Though she was sincere in her offers of help, she hoped the occasional phone call and get-together would be all the support her friend needed from her. Beneath the veneer of bravado, she was as questioning as Jill.

* * *

Once on Highway 20, the drive was easy. Jill even got into the correct lane at the Dorval Circle. But despite it being a Sunday evening, there was construction under the arc lights, and she forgot her concerns while she concentrated on navigating through the lane and turning detours.

It was only after she had safely parked the car and headed for the arrivals concourse, that she asked herself how she'd greet her husband. She had almost twenty minutes to answer that question and to plan the direction she wanted their first conversation to go. They had to agree on what the boys should be told. More important to Jill was discovering whether Brad had someone else. To separate or to try to recapture his affection hinged on the answer to that question.

Chapter 32
Farewells and What-ifs

6:40 p.m., Sunday, October 25th
Stanfield International Airport, outside Halifax

For a moment, Kate felt pleased she had gotten her way in their first disagreement. Why on earth would Brad think she would want to say a hurried farewell at the drop-off area outside the departure entrance to the airport? It wasn't so much that she had won the argument as the fact that she, the driver, had determined where the car would go.

After they parked, Brad checked in and they had time for a coffee and an uncomfortable conversation. Neither knew whether fate, in all its entanglements, would get in the way of their continuing liaison. She certainly hadn't wanted that to be goodbye but was fearful it might be.

While she did not wish to broach the "is this our separation occasion?" topic, it was foremost in her mind. And then it was time.

She dumped their garbage while Brad collected his carry-on baggage, and they walked hand-in-hand the short walk to the security entrance. There was no line-up. Brad set down his bags and wrapped his arms around her.

Tight against him, she wished his arms would never let her go. She pushed him away ever so slightly when he laughed. "Is that you laughing, Brad? I'm glad you find something amusing in this situation. Tell me what it is. Perhaps it will keep the tears away."

"I'm sorry," he said. "But I've just seen the irony of this moment. It was so easy to put down my baggage so I could enfold you and comfort you. And where am I going and what am I going to do? I'm headed home to cast off my baggage so I can do those things to you and for you forever. I wish that would be as easy."

She burst into tears and wrapped her arms around him tighter, burying her face to hide the tears. But her body was wracked in sobs that she could not conceal.

* * *

Brad didn't know, or care, whether it was a time for words or speeches because he had things he needed to say. He wanted to comfort this woman, whom he'd grown so fond of in less than two days. He couldn't do anything but hug her. Words and promises were all he had left.

He promised he would do all he could to come back to her. He promised he would do all he could to free himself. He promised he would not make any rash or premature moves; in fact, he would not do anything that affected her without first consulting her. She would know every development, and hopefully they would all be positive. But she had the right to know if things went wrong, too.

He wasn't sure how much of this Kate took in, but the sobbing had finished before he reached the part he had planned for this stage. "Kate, I have to leave you now," was his beginning of the end. "When you let go of me, you should know that I'm thinking I'm in love with you. If I was twenty, I'd be positive. At my age, I know differently. It's too quick, but I do know I want to be with you, so it's goodbye until the next time."

He felt her arms relax. She stepped back. "I've been avoiding the 'L' word even though I wanted to use it and hear it. Like you say, it's too soon. We'll have to wait and see. Now go—and don't look back. I'm leaving, too."

Brad watched her turn, avoiding his attempt to entice her into a farewell kiss. He thought he saw her pull a tissue from her coat pocket and wipe her eyes. True to her promise, she did not turn around.

* * *

"I must look a mess," Kate muttered, when she stopped to pay for parking at the carpark entrance. Tears had been streaming down her face for at least five minutes. She had control of her emotions, but her tears gave her away. She had never found airports upsetting. Until now, her experiences there had been positive.

The thoughts were intermingled with the emotional content and came at her fast and furious. That expression seemed apt. The "furious" ones were mostly of the "what-if" variety. She refused to acknowledge those. Or did she?

Almost subconsciously, she drove the highway back to the city. The roads were dry, the weather was clear, and the Sunday evening traffic was light. Her mind was not on the road. Instead it filtered thoughts as speculation. What if that Jill woman wouldn't let him go? Would she have one or two stepsons? Conundrums such as these could only be answered by future events—hopefully not too far in the future.

For the positives, Kate feasted on his promises, one being that he'd call and report on the next day's talks. And then she had to wrack her memory to recall if he'd specified a time. Just like her to be wallowing in the bath when he phoned. Then she remembered it was one of those "I'll phone when I can" arrangements.

Then came pondering: *If everything turns out positive, how long will it take?* The only answer she could give was a vague "long time." This, of course, led to what was almost another "what-if," but not quite, question. *At what stage in the proceedings of Brad splitting from his wife can I become involved with him again?*

The latter question produced a smile when she realized another form of asking that question: *When can I jump back into bed with him?* The smile vanished, and she shuddered. Could this past weekend's activities, if they came to light, be used by Jill as grounds for divorce and all that was entailed in the apportioning of blame?

The turn off the highway broke her train of thought. It was not yet eight. Jenny would be chomping at the bit for details of the fond farewells. Kate steeled herself for a confrontation until she realized that, for the second time that day, personal conversations with her growing daughter could be both pleasurable and comforting. But the "L" word would not feature in the conversation. What she experienced felt like love, but as a male acquaintance had once said, "So does a good donair washed down with Keith's draught."

She pulled into her underground parking spot and repaired her makeup. When she exited the car, heading for normality, her final thought was, *If everything turns out right and hurdles go down, what I feel for Brad will definitely become love.*

Jenny opened the condo door while Kate rummaged in her purse for the key.

"Oh, I was hoping you'd bring a pizza," were not the first words Kate hoped she would hear from her daughter on such a significant return.

Chapter 33
Right and Wrong?

8:45 p.m., Sunday, October 25th
Pierre Elliot Trudeau International Airport, Dorval, Montreal

Jill successfully negotiated the roadworks around the terminal and even found a convenient parking spot. She was early and enquired where passengers from Halifax would be emerging. If anyone from the Montreal office had been with Brad, she might recognize the woman when they came through. But surely Brad wouldn't be stupid enough to walk off the plane with his woman, knowing Jill was there to meet him.

The only familiar passenger was Brad, who was alone. His eyes sought her among the welcoming crowd, and he waved when he spotted her. Surprisingly, he made no move to avoid the welcoming kiss she planned. But there was no passion in his tentative embrace or the brief touching of their lips.

She stepped back, looked her husband straight in the eye, and spoke part two of the plan she'd hastily put together while waiting in the arrivals concourse.

Brad's expression, as her words hit home, told her all she needed to know. Taking the initiative, she announced, "Brad, before we start any discussion, I need you to know that I want us to try again; that is, unless you have somebody else."

Her husband was seldom stuck for words. All she saw was an open mouth below eyes that blinked and refused to meet hers. He bent to retrieve his bags, mumbling. When he straightened, he suggested they find a bar and get a drink while they talked. He hastily added, "I don't think we'll have long enough to sort out essentials if we drive straight home to the boys."

She agreed. More time to discover this "someone" her husband was seeing. Her intuition was reinforced by Brad's unwillingness to meet her gaze.

* * *

Brad had to stall. He, too, had his opening strategy planned, but Jill had struck first, and her statements countered his. His opening gambit of "This marriage is damaged beyond repair, and it's time to go our separate ways" had been scuttled.

He was thankful for the stalling time when Jill agreed to go for a drink. They found a bar on the departure level. She asked for a large gin and tonic while he had a beer.

He guessed the long delay in his response to her statement would not sit comfortably with her. Her "Do I need to say it again?" was an indicator of her impatience. He deliberately said nothing, out-waiting her when she repeated, "Can we try again, or is there somebody else? I sense that there might be because you didn't deny it."

He decided to stick with his original plan and said, "I've been doing a lot of thinking this weekend, Jill. I believe our marriage is too damaged to retrieve. I think we need to agree to separate and sit down and work out the details."

She leaned toward him as though about to stand and go nose-to-nose with him across the round table. His wife's body language, no matter what form it took, always preceded an attack. His first thought was that the quick fix wasn't going to happen when she vehemently persisted with, "I asked first. Is there someone else? Are you hiding something? At least I was up front about Aaron. Be a man and stop hiding her from me."

He couldn't stop himself. He went off on a tangent that added fuel to the probable conflagration. "And how long had you been meeting with Aaron before you had to tell me because you knew I'd found out?"

"History, Brad! History. Aaron and I are finished. He was using me, probably the same way you're using your fancy piece. But at least I had the sense to give him up for the sake of the boys and our marriage."

Brad knew she was lying. "You told me earlier that he'd dumped you, so stop trying to play the good guy in this mess. You strayed first, Jill, and now you want to come crawling back as though it never happened."

He'd erred. She hadn't missed his mistake.

"First? Did you say 'first,' Brad? That means you strayed, too. That's why you want out, isn't it?" She signaled to the bartender for a refill.

"I want out because I can't live this way. Neither of us trusts the other. We can't keep pretending—or, I can't. But then you've had more practice than me. It's over, Jill. Let's face up to it and try to do what's right for the boys and stop throwing blame around like this."

"That would suit you and your woman, wouldn't it? A quickie divorce so you two can set up and play house and have happy families while I bring up James alone."

He had to prevent the pitched battle that was close. But how? The accusations and anger would be followed by tears and "Oh, pity me." From past experience, he knew his wife could employ the full gamut of emotions. She'd done so before when she negotiated, continuing with Aaron after Brad had found out about him. The last two ridiculous years Jill had lost herself in fitness, lunches out, shopping, afternoon wine drinking, and other activities that had led to Aaron. She hadn't wanted Brad. She'd neglected him. They occupied separate beds. Only token affection and history remained. And the boys, of course.

He engineered a long silence, aided by the arrival of drinks. He was trying to plan and re-strategize before Jill began again. He didn't know if he was saying the right thing or making a costly confession when he blurted, "I did meet someone this weekend, but that's not why I want out of our marriage. It's over, Jill. Whether I've met someone or—"

"You prefer her to me, and that's what this is all about. Is she from here? Someone at work? I'll find out and you can have your separation, but the divorce is going to cost you—and not just money. Let's finish here and go tell the boys their mom and dad are divorcing."

Her voice was carrying to neighbouring tables, and his discomfort urged him to abandon the public area and continue the discussion later. He got up, walked to the bar, and settled the tab while Jill either became angrier or calmed down.

Hopefully the walk to the car would allow her more time to cool off.

* * *

Jill was eager to begin her cross-examination to discover who Brad had met, but he left to pay the bill. She downed her gin and tonic. He was right. The marriage was over. If he had found someone else, there was no hope. But he'd said something like, "I met someone this weekend," which meant it was still casual, a weekender. *Time to play cool*, she thought. *I have to find out about this woman.*

He returned just as she'd finished composing herself. She suggested they go the slow way home and find somewhere to park so they could agree on exactly what to tell the boys. She led them to the car and let him drive.

Once he'd navigated out of the airport congestion, they headed toward the river. After he parked, she turned on the contrite act, saying, "If you have someone else, then maybe you're right. We're finished. We can talk separation. But you say you just met her this weekend. She must be special if she's made this much impact on you."

She thought she'd caught him off guard when he started, "She is and—" But he caught himself on the brink of her trap.

"No, Jill. If anything comes of this, you'll find out. When you and I make some decisions, then I'll be back in touch with her. Sorry, that's all I'm saying. You may be collecting ammunition for later."

She snickered. "You got that right! Tell me about her," she persisted.

"Can't do that. She will only come into the picture if and when we split up."

"You mean if we stay together, she's out?"

"No, Jill, I mean we should separate. Yes, I know, I didn't have to go on all those work trips, but you probably knew that. And aren't you surprised that Harry didn't wonder what was happening between us long before this weekend? Our marriage is a sham. You have to agree on that."

"It has been, but I think we can salvage something if I promise not to go gallivanting. I can spend more time with you. Maybe I can accompany you on your business trips. We need a vacation—together. We can go to marriage counselling. Honestly, Aaron has finished with me, and I'm never going that route again. I want to settle back down. It's worth a try, don't you think?"

Brad broke the long silence. Twice he stuttered in an attempt to respond but succeeded on his third attempt. "I want to believe you, Jill."

She thought for a moment that he was agreeable to a reconciliation until he continued. Two short sentences. Nine words. "It's too late. And I think I'm in love."

She wanted to shout, *No, you're not! You just think you are! You're acting like a seventeen-year-old who's just had his first weekend of sex. Get real!* Instead, she demanded he take her home. "I don't care what you tell the boys as long as they know that this is what you want. You can deal with the hate and blame Harry's been throwing at me all weekend. You can explain to James why his dad hasn't come home to fix things but wants to make them worse."

She turned her back on him and slumped into the seat, hoping he could hear her sobs when he started the car.

Part Two

RETURN TO REALITY

Life would be simple if you could always make plans that work.
But the present is not only determined by a disordered past,
it faces an unknown future.
The heart, too, is unpredictable.

Chapter 34
Pacifying and Protocols

10:00 p.m., Sunday, October 25th
Treetops Terrace, Kirkland, Montreal

Jill knew she couldn't deal with the boys and Brad right away. To her surprise, Brad agreed. They had almost acted like a happily married couple when they'd come through the door. Jill had taken the initiative, explaining to the boys that she and their father had a lot to discuss and would be taking tomorrow off work to see what they could sort out.

Harry's only comment was, "Good luck with that!"

When she and Brad had made it clear the boys wouldn't be involved in discussions until the following evening, James pronounced, "That's not fair," at which point Harry reached over and tousled his brother's hair, saying, "Smart kid, my brother."

James brushed him away, and she invited her youngest to sit beside her.

Despite Harry's body language indicating otherwise, both boys agreed their parents needed time to work out what should be done. The boys wanted to know what "the situation" was. Brad deferred to her, as they exchanged glances.

Jill was relieved, and surprised, that Brad didn't correct or add to her simplistic explanation. Harry had a look of disbelief when she finished explaining that she and Brad had drifted apart and needed to decide whether to stay together or separate. Either way, they loved their sons and wanted to do what was best for them. James' questions looked for explanations and instant solutions. To her relief, Harry persuaded his brother to leave the talking to the grown-ups. If they did that, they might have answers after school the next day.

Harry shrugged off her mother's maternal hand that rested on his as a token of thanks.

* * *

After the boys had been ushered upstairs, Brad asked if he and Jill should lay out ground rules for the next morning.

Brad thought the silence might be a calm-before-a-Jill-explosion, but she came back with, "We'll have to try to control our emotions." He was relieved they were in agreement and Jill was being positive.

She added, "You know how much harder that is for me."

He jumped in, perhaps a little prematurely, failing to praise her for her insight. "We have to be reasonable, both of us. And we can't react or revisit recent history. Look what happened coming from the airport. We'll only get into mud-slinging, and there's been enough of that, real and imagined, to start world war three."

"What do you mean, 'imagined'?" Her voice increased a notch, and she leaned forward in her chair. "I might have speculated about your Halifax whore but—" She covered her mouth.

They slumped back into their chairs, looking askance at each other. The silence buzzed in Brad's ears.

Jill broke the silence. "Sorry. We also have to avoid the 'blame game' if we are to try to make sense of this. Don't you agree?"

"Yeah, we've got to. How about this"—Brad, the planner, almost felt as comfortable as in a business meeting—"if either of us feel that something the other says is an attack that will lead to mud-slinging or a blaming game, we raise a hand. That means we both walk away and take a break. Doesn't matter what we do. Walk around the house, grab a coffee, bathroom break, grab a beer, pour a glass of wine. Even smoke a cigarette, if you've started up again—"

He raised his hand. "Sorry. I know how hard you worked to quit." He sighed. "When did we get into the habit of making snide comments at one another? It's almost second nature. We've got to stop that, too."

"It could work," Jill agreed. "And it will keep us constructive instead of saying things that helped destroy our marriage."

His yawn cut off further discussion. "I don't know about you, but I'm too tired to get into this tonight. Got to wake up early and cancel my afternoon meeting."

"I thought the meeting was in Halifax and that's why you had to stay."

He thought quickly. "It was a conference call. I'm more relevant and I have more local information when I'm in the Halifax office."

Before she could question him further, he added, "Let's get some sleep. Is the bed made up in the spare room?"

When they stood, she touched his elbow. "There's still your half of the king next to me. I'd like it if you took that instead of the 'dog house' spare room."

He responded quickly. "I don't think so. I'm not being nasty when I say you might try to prejudice tomorrow's negotiations if I accept your invitation." He turned and checked the lights and doors.

"Too exhausted after your weekend with your bit-on-the-side?" Jill asked.

Brad cringed and collected his luggage. Would she ever give up?

Chapter 35
Negotiating and Mothering

11:00 a.m., Monday, October 26th
Treetops Terrace, Kirkland, Montreal

The phone rang at 11:00 a.m., interrupting an impasse. Brad was adamant the marriage was irretrievably broken, whereas Jill was certain that, given changes they could make, it could be repaired. They had been trying to define those changes, with Brad trying to convince his wife that it was too late. They had been talking, with no real argument, for two hours. The restraint she had shown the previous night before they'd disappeared to their separate rooms continued. That, in itself, was remarkable given the resentments and bottled-up, confused emotions they each held. Despite that, anger remained on a leash, threatening to escape on a number of occasions, and they'd each raised their hands twice when something that threatened the new accord was said. Four brief pauses had scarcely delayed sensible discussion.

Brad retrieved Jill's I-phone from the table. Her cursory check caused her to swear. "It's James' school. I'd better take it."

Most of the conversation came from the school, with Jill interjecting affirmative grunts until it concluded with her saying, "I'm home, so I can be there to collect him in ten minutes." She rolled her eyes at Brad, and he suddenly remembered that amongst information given to the boys the previous evening, nobody had defined the elusive "things" that were going to be sorted out.

After the phone call, Jill assumed her concerned-mother role. "James has had his head down on his desk in both classes this morning. He says he's been throwing up, but that may not be true. When he was brought to the office, he said he wanted to go home, that he was too upset to be in class. Then he burst into tears. I think it's best if I go get him."

Brad concurred, adding that once James was calmed down, they could resume their conversation.

As Jill donned her jacket and looked for her car keys, he said, "At least we know we can talk sensibly and constructively even when there are so many things to be sorted. James is just one of them. You tell him what you think he needs to know. But make sure he knows all four of us are talking after dinner. We have to hear from them and offer reassurance, whatever we decide."

"Gotta go," she said. The door closed and then, abruptly, reopened. "And I meant to tell you. I haven't started to smoke again, but boy am I tempted. How about you?" She grinned and stuck out her tongue.

Brad laughed. Humour was a change from the criticism and sniping that had become venomous in past weeks.

* * *

Jill found her son, dressed and ready to go home, outside the school office. When she went to comfort him, the school secretary appeared. "He won't tell me what it is, but something is making him unhappy."

Jill formed her best parental smile and asked if she could talk to the principal. She hated to air her problems but felt someone at school should know why her baby was going through a bad time.

Ten minutes later, while James sat in the outer office, Jill was reassured by Ms. Graham that she understood and that James could ask to see her anytime he was upset. Ms. Graham confided to Jill that she and her kids had gone through a separation and divorce a couple of years previously, so she knew what it could do to teenagers. "Tell him to see me as soon as he gets to school tomorrow. I'll let his teachers know to keep an eye on him, but be assured I won't tell them why."

As Jill headed home with James, she was aware that sharing her major concern—James' reaction to whatever happened between her and Brad—had brought a sense of relief. Chrissie was one ally, but Ms. Graham could be another.

"Had a nice talk with your principal. It's nice to know someone at school is there to—"

"Ms. Graham's usually a witch, but today she was okay."

Jill laughed. "She's your friend now, James, and understands why you were upset today."

Inside the house, she was amused that she'd compared her new ally with Chrissie. What would happen if they both offered conflicting advice at the same time? Jill sensed that beneath the tightly wrapped Ms. Graham was a person who'd relate to Chrissie. A vision of the principal smoking dope with Chrissie flashed before her.

* * *

Anticipating a hungry son coming home early from school, Brad prepared tuna sandwiches for lunch. But James was more interested in talking to his parents than eating. Brad explained that no one would be talking until they had all eaten. Even Jill, in support of husband and son, forced down a not-too-dainty sandwich that was clearly in conflict with her diet and the day's missed exercise class.

Brad wasn't sure he liked the school principal knowing of their marital problems, but he understood when Jill explained why she had confided in the woman. Later, she added that Ms. Graham had been through a similar experience with her own sons. James added his five cents, saying it was good someone at school knew as long as it wasn't the other kids.

Brad realized that James thought he could join in the discussions when he asked, "What did you and Mom decide this morning?"

Jill stepped in with the right words, explaining these big problems needed time before they could be fixed and that James would have to wait to see what had been decided. It wouldn't be fair to Harry if James were in on a discussion without his brother.

Once again, Brad had the pleasant experience, not only of agreeing with his wife but feeling good at how she expressed their opinions. He had forgotten how much better she was at communicating with their youngest.

* * *

James, knowing he wasn't getting much news from his parents, escaped to his room. He turned on a video game, purposely turning the sound louder than usual. Leaving his bedroom door open, he sneaked to the top of the stairs, sat down, and strained to hear what his parents were saying.

Suddenly, his mother shouted, "This isn't fair, James. You agreed and now you're spying on us. Please go to your room and shut the door."

"Aw, Mom. It's you and Dad that aren't fair. How can I play a game when I'm thinking about you guys?"

His mother appeared at the bottom of the stairs. "Perhaps we should go to my office or Dad's to sort things out. Would you prefer that?"

He slunk back to his room, slamming the door. He turned up the volume as high as it could go.

And then his father barged in. "Now who's not being fair?"

James fell to the bed. He'd leave them alone if that's what they wanted. And everything would end well.

* * *

Jill's heart was not in the discussions, a fact she admitted to Brad early afternoon. She added, "Let's just summarise what we have agreed to and talk that over with the boys when Harry gets in."

She really had no answer to Brad's question, "And where we don't agree?"

"I'm sure you can draw up two lists, Brad." She could not resist the dig. Brad loved his lists. *Good luck compiling a list of what we agree on.*

Brad had his tablet out ready, so she said, "It's far too complex for agree/disagree lists, Brad."

To her amazement, her husband concurred because he suggested the boys be told they were still trying to come to some agreement.

It was only as Jill was headed for the gym before Harry came home that she realized Brad had drawn back from his rigid stance that separation was the only solution.

* * *

***I** should have known,* Harry thought, as his brother was ushered off to bed. Out loud, he said to his parents, "So nothing has been decided, then? You're going round in circles talking. Dad wants out, but Mom wants to keep on trying."

His father pleaded. "It's not that simple, son."

From the depths of his mother's armchair, Harry heard her mumble, "It might be if you gave up your Halifax woman."

"Don't go there, Jill," his father quickly interjected.

"Did I hear right? Dad's got somebody else?" Harry asked.

"Ask him!" His mother sat up, showing enthusiasm for the first time in the after-supper discussions.

"You need to understand, Harry, that she has nothing to do with your mom and I separating. That all started a couple of years ago," his father argued defensively.

"You mean you've had this woman for two years, hidden away?" Harry said.

His mother laughed.

"What's so amusing in this, Mom? Did you know?"

"Oh, Harry! Your father could never keep a secret for two years. What's so funny is that he says he only met her this weekend." She looked at his father for a response.

"It's true, Harry, so Kate has nothing to do with your mom and I splitting up."

This time it was Harry's turn to laugh. "So you meet this woman and tell Mom over the phone that you want out and you say there's no connection? Give me a break!"

As Harry grabbed his jacket, he heard his father claim that it hadn't happened that way. Harry slammed the door when he left.

* * *

Jill followed Harry, ignoring Brad's advice to let him be. She looked both ways up the darkened street but could see no one, so she took the path to the back deck.

"Harry, you here?" she called, looking in the shadows on the deck.

"Over here, Mom," came Harry's voice from the lounger.

"Sorry I laughed, Harry, but you see why, don't you?"

"Yeah, and it beats you crying any day."

She dragged a chair next to her son. "Sorry," was all she could offer.

There was no response until a quiet voice said, "It's the unknown, Mom. I can't deal with what I don't know."

Jill reached over to tousle Harry's hair. "Once James is settled, your dad and I will talk some more. No instant solutions to promise."

"I know, Mom. I'll sit here for a while and text a few people. Get my mind off things."

"I'll go tell Dad because I know he'll be worrying what's happened to both of us." With that, Jill let herself back into the house and promised herself she would look for a solution, not laughter.

Chapter 36
First Report From the Peace Negotiations

9:30 p.m., Monday, October 26th
Phone call from Treetops Terrace, Kirkland, to West Condos, Halifax

After Brad returned to the kitchen from settling down James, he told Jill he had a phone call to make before they resumed discussions.

"It's to her, isn't it?" Jill asked, with that timbre in her voice that hinted at angry emotion. Brad was surprised she'd kept it under control.

"Yes, it is. I promised I'd report on events after I got home. She knows we planned to spend the day trying to sort out our future."

Without thinking, he blurted, "I don't mind you sitting here while we talk. That way you'll know I'm being straight with you."

As fast as he'd spoken the words, the regrets came even faster. He glanced at Jill, hoping she'd turn him down. Instead, she said, "I'll have to go and say goodnight to James and make sure he knows it's back to school tomorrow. Won't be long, then I can listen in to your conversation."

She grinned, turning her expression to that of someone who'd secured a victory. "How lucky can I get? How many women get permission to listen to their husband talking with his mistress? It's almost kinky." She flounced up the stairs, shouting a goodnight to Harry's closed door. Seconds later, Brad heard her muffled voice, presumably in James' room.

He pushed Kate's number, surprised how quickly she answered.

"About time, Brad. I start my shift at seven tomorrow morning and was hoping for an early night. I've been waiting for your call. What happened?"

He tried to diffuse her impatience. "I'm sorry, Kate. We've been talking the best part of eight hours, first Jill and I and, since supper, the boys joined in. First chance I've had to call."

Did he need to tell Kate what he'd decided? "Listen, I told Jill she could hear what I had to report to you on the phone. Not my best idea, but I—"

The phone exploded in his ear. "YOU DID WHAT, BRAD? PLEASE TELL ME WE'RE NOT ON SPEAKER PHONE. FUCK, BRAD. WHAT ARE YOU PLANNING BACK THERE, A MENAGE A TROIS?"

Before Brad interjected, Kate continued "No, don't answer that. I won't share you, Brad, not even on a long distance phone call. Tell that to Jill, and call me tomorrow. And stop trying to be the nice guy to everyone. It's impossible! I'll be home by four tomorrow, your time."

Still holding the phone, he looked up to see Jill had returned.

"True love not running smoothly, sweetheart?"

"You could say that," he said. "She wants me to call back tomorrow, but she doesn't want you listening."

"Surprise! Surprise! Maybe now you realize trying to be Mr. Nice Guy ever since you got home had to rebound on you."

"I will never understand what women want. I try so hard to give it to them."

"Yeah, right. Here's another one for you, husband of mine. Seeing as your Halifax lady has turned you down, the right-hand side of my bed is still open for you. Comfort and consolation await. You can celebrate a whole day without a row—with me, that is. And you can take that any way you want to."

He was tired of her sarcasm.

Halfway up the stairs, she turned and stared at him.

Unbelievable! Was she waiting for an answer? Did she really think he'd accept her invitation? "Nice try, Jill. Again, I think you're looking to prejudice negotiations. And they went well even if we can't agree."

"Will . . . um, oh . . . tell me her name, otherwise she'll just be your Halifax Whore."

"Her name is Kate," he said, suddenly realizing he had given away what might be a strategic piece of information.

Jill continued slowly up the stairs and then turned. "And will Kate be thinking negotiations went well today, Brad? Did you win, or did you lose? Or did you just blow it by trying to please both of us?" She raised her hand in the air giving the victory sign, which morphed into a "follow me" beckoning of the index finger.

He ignored her and plopped on the couch. When he went upstairs ten minutes later, he passed by Jill's open door without even a "goodnight" glance. He lay in bed wondering why, in those before-bed exchanges, Jill had reverted to her old sarcastic, demeaning self. And this after they had agreed on so much. For a moment, he wavered in his belief that the marriage was doomed, wondering whether to visit Jill in their room.

Then he realized that would be victory for Jill's argument for reconciliation.

Chapter 37
Advice and Mothering

11:30 a.m., Tuesday, October 27th
Phone from Treetops Terrace, Kirkland, to Beaconsfield

Jill and Brad put on brave faces while Brad readied to go to the office and she helped the boys prepare for school. She and Brad weren't certain James would last the entire day but had decided he should get back into his routine. James agreed, adding that he hoped his parents would talk more that evening and set things right.

Neither Brad nor Jill could define an agreed meaning for that phrase. Neither, they assumed, could the boys.

After Brad left for work, Jill puttered around, had a leisurely shower, and by 11:30 a.m. assumed she would not be receiving a come-rescue-your-son phone call.

Time to call Chrissie, she thought, and give her the two pieces of bad news.

"You were right, Chrissie. He does have someone else. He's met this woman in Halifax. The good news is that he was foolish enough to give me her name last night. I'll get more out of him when he gets home from work today."

"That's good," Chrissie said. "And is the other bad news that now he's got this other woman he wants a divorce? Because if that's the situation, you need a lawyer to give this woman's name to."

Jill wasn't pleased to hear the bluntness in Chrissie's appraisal of the situation and tried to minimise it. "Well, we haven't come up with the 'D' word in our talks. Best we've mentioned, I think, is legal separation. I guess that's this evening's topic. For sure, he wants out."

"I guess the femme fatale seduction ploy didn't work then?"

Another blunt statement from the astute friend caused Jill to evaluate her strategy. She rubbed her eyes and sighed. "I couldn't have spelled it out any clearer if I'd done the dance of the seven veils on the dining table. No, cold-fish Brad wouldn't play."

"Got a pen and paper? I'll give you my lawyer's name and number. When you call him, tell him I referred you. He's good, and now I think you're going to need him."

Jill was regretting the conversation with Chrissie, which forced her to face up to the reality of her situation. Nevertheless, she took the details from her friend. Then she told the story of Brad expecting his Halifax hussy to allow Jill to listen to their phone conversation. Jill and Chrissie laughed. Neither could decide whether Brad was just plain stupid, naïve, or had no understanding, at all, of women.

* * *

When Jill finally hung up, Chrissie wondered if she had gotten herself too deep into what was about to turn into a quagmire. *Too late now,* she thought. I *offered help and support, so I have to follow through.*

She paused, recalling the trauma of her own marriage breakup, memories she'd been trying to forget. She did not envy Jill's next few months. Poor woman. She might think she knew what was coming, but she wouldn't until it was all over. And in the end, you hate what the situation forced you to become.

She poured herself the first glass of wine of the day and then phoned around to see if anything was happening with her friends. Best she could find was a lunch gathering at a restaurant, which would not have been her choice. She invited herself along anyway. She didn't relish spending the day alone with thoughts of her past that Jill's call had provoked. Later in the day, she'd work on company for the evening.

* * *

Jill decided against contacting Chrissie's lawyer. If the evening conversation and Brad's call to—what was her name?—Kate indicated there was no hope of reconciliation, she'd call the lawyer the next day. That is, if she could bring herself to do so. Maybe it was still too early. But what if she left it too late and Brad made the "lawyer" move before she did?

Life would be so much simpler if Brad had agreed the marriage was worth saving. Then they could start to work on saving it.

And what was this Kate like? What did Brad see in her? Had it started before this last weekend? He seemed to have been visiting Halifax quite a lot. Had he been seeing her for longer, or was that her imagination working overtime? Too many unknowns.

Thoughts kept milling round. She had to get away from the whirlwind for a few hours. A drive to Hudson to spend time with her mother would do it—if her mother was home.

Jill reached for her phone. As soon as she'd made the arrangements, more "what-ifs" arrived, led by "What if mother wheedles the situation from her?" Her mother had expertise from years of practice at that maternal skill.

Chapter 38
Tension and Relaxation

3:45 p.m., Tuesday, October 27th
Cafe Italiano, Kirkland Centre, Kirkland

Harry was only too happy when someone suggested a coffee before they split after their day in classes at CEGEP. He should get home to see if James was less confused and moody than the previous day, in case their mother wasn't home when he returned from school. Perhaps a more responsible attitude and her desire to stick together as a family would promote changes.

All day, his thoughts kept reverting to the entrenched attitude his father had displayed the previous evening. His father wouldn't consider his wife's belief that their marriage could and should be saved to keep them as a united family. When his mother had let slip that this "other woman" was an issue, his father had interjected far too quickly and loudly with, "Don't go there yet, Jill."

Nothing had been determined from the prior night's discussion, and he wondered if anything would change at home today. He was in no hurry to get back there. His too-organised father had set 6:30 p.m. as a time to start the talks again. How many other families resolved problems with business-like family meetings? Not many, he guessed.

His pondering was disturbed by a question whispered in his ear by Lynsey, when she leaned into him, wrapped her arm around his neck, and pulled him down to her lips.

* * *

Lynsey was bothered by Harry's distance, almost as if he wasn't there. Usually, he was front and centre in the back and forth exchanges of their group. Today—nothing! Not a word after the curt "Sounds good" when it was suggested he go with them for coffee. Lynsey wondered if this would be an opportunity to get closer to the guy to whom she was attracted.

She'd already pushed her way next to him on the bench in the booth. With the buzz of three or four conversations going on around them, she snugged closer, reached up, and pulled his ear to meet her mouth. "What's wrong, Harry? You're way too quiet. Anything I can do?" She whispered, not caring about the "looks" she got from others in the group.

No response, but he didn't pull away, even when he let out a huge sigh. Had she mistaken his silence for what was really indifference toward her? She'd been making it clear for the last couple of weeks that she wanted to know him better, but he hadn't taken the bait.

He shifted and bent his head toward hers. "Problems at home between my parents. It's a mess, and I don't know what's happening."

She still had her arm around his neck, so she pulled him closer as a sign of sympathy. "Want to go somewhere and talk about it? I have my mom's car. We could take a drive."

"Sure," he said.

She was pleased he agreed quickly, without time to consider. He must like her, after all.

They pushed their way out of the booth. She gripped his hand, afraid he might change his mind.

She started the Honda. "Where to?" Without waiting for an answer, she said, "There's nobody home at my place. Wanna go there?" Quickly, she added, "To talk."

Harry laughed. "I've been dreaming of such an invite since we started hanging out together. But right now my life is so screwed up . . . I don't know . . ." His mood immediately switched back to the silent confusion from which she was trying to save him.

* * *

Harry should have found it easy to respond to an invitation from a young woman with whom he was intensely attracted. Easier still when the invitation was to her empty house. "Talking" was the most used euphemism in the English language—so they'd heard in class the previous week.

It didn't make sense that the opportunity to talk to someone, to tell someone what was happening with his family, was more appealing than going to Lynsey's place to "talk," or whatever they would do if he wasn't so fucked up at the moment.

He told this to Lynsey on the short drive to her house, three streets over from his.

She giggled. "If you need to talk, talk. I understand. When my brother left home last year, our family was messed up, so I know something of what you're going through. No right answers, correct?"

"You got that right!" he responded.

Lynsey smiled, opened the door, and led him into the empty house.

* * *

Time was a factor, and Lynsey wasn't sure what to tell Harry. She warned him that her mother would be home at five and that she wasn't supposed to have boys in the house when her parents weren't home.

She sympathized with Harry's mother, who seemed to want to put things right even though her behaviour had started it all. His dad sounded like a bossy male who wouldn't bend one bit and who might even have a girlfriend somewhere. She shared these opinions with Harry before she offered to run him home.

As Harry collected his jacket and books, she had an idea. "I know how uptight you are with this. When my brother and parents were fighting, which made my mom and dad fight even more, my other brother helped me. Wait a minute!"

She raced upstairs to her room, remembering where she had hidden the emergency stash from her helpful brother.

Back downstairs, she handed Harry a pair of socks.

"What's this?" he asked.

She snatched them from his hands and unrolled them to reveal two joints. "When you get as desperate as you were before you unloaded on me, try smoking one of these. No, what am I saying. Don't smoke it all, you'll be right out of it—unless you already use."

"Only a couple of times at parties," he replied. "Thanks for this, Lynsey. And thanks for letting me talk to you about it."

"If you need to talk more tonight, I'll be here. Now let's get out of here before we meet my mom in the driveway. We could maybe do this tomorrow?"

Harry's reply, "Don't see why not," were the best words she'd heard all day.

Chapter 39
Dumped and Recovering

4:00 p.m., Tuesday, October 27th
Phone from Highway Condos, Bedford, to West Condos, Halifax

When the phone rang, Jenny assumed it was her mom. She often called at the end of her shift, sometimes to say she had to shop or was going for coffee with one of her friends. Jenny was usually more interested in hearing what her mother would be preparing for dinner. But there were more significant happenings in her mother's life, and therefore hers, too, than dinner, so she answered the phone without checking the display, "What's happening, Mom? Anything new?"

She was taken aback when her father's voice replied, "I don't know. Should there be something?"

"Sorry, Dad. Should have looked to see who it was first. Just waiting for Mom to bring home dinner." She shifted focus. "What's with you? Anything from Suzie?"

"That's why I'm calling. Buddy next door phoned to say stuff was being moved out of our condo. I left work early to check it out. Suzie's been back and taken all her things—everything. Buddy said there was a guy helping her load up two cars. She's gone, Jen."

"Oh, Dad, I'm so sorry. I hate you being by yourself."

"After the last conversation, I don't think your mom wants me back either. But, kiddo, look on the bright side. You can visit, and you'll be able to sleep without interruption."

"Do you know where she went? Did she leave a note?"

"Yes. She wanted to let me know she was safe. She met this guy in The Horse and Groom downtown, and he's offered her a room in his house in Cowie Hill. So . . . that's it, except she said she must have a thing for older men because he's older than me. I thought I'd give it a couple of days and then phone her."

Jenny didn't think that was a good idea but kept her opinion to herself. "Poor Daddy. It's Mom's weekend at work, so I can spend time with you, perhaps. I'll check it out with her. Or do you have plans?"

"No, I have no plans. Except there's this woman at work I should try to date. She's more my age."

"Dad, you're hopeless. Give it a rest! Oh, here's Mom. I'll phone you about the weekend later. Bye."

* * *

Mike put his phone on the coffee table and looked at the mess Suzie had left. He knew what he'd be doing this evening. But first he was hungry and might as well eat before he started. Beer and pub food at the Riverside would help him feel less isolated. It had been good to hear his daughter's voice. A weekend with her would be better than bar hopping and looking for another Suzie, which was all he ever seemed to find these days.

He bent down to pick up empty coat hangers strewn over the bedroom floor, but quickly gave up. He grabbed his jacket and decided to get Janice's phone number at work the next day. *I think I'm getting the right message from her. I hope so, anyway. I'll see if she's on Facebook later.*

Positive thoughts were interrupted. "Did that bitch, Suzie, take my laptop?"

He returned to the chaos of the bedroom and there it was, under his pillow. He breathed a sigh of relief and muttered, "Lots to do, but beer and a burger come first. But only one beer."

* * *

"Hi, Mom, how was your day?" Jenny asked. Before her mother could answer, she relayed her father's call and the news that Suzie had moved out. He'd gotten the message her mother had given him. "And do you believe he's already looking for another girlfriend?"

"Another twenty-year-old I expect," her mother said.

"No, Mom. He thinks a woman at work, who's about his age, is checking him out. You know Dad. He won't be lonely for long."

"Lovely. I know that man's propensity to wander."

"Big words, Mom. But how about your wandering—singular, that is. Anything from Brad? I heard you from my room. Can't have been good if he got you cussing."

"Nothing to tell. He's calling soon to report on what's happened since he got home on Sunday. He wanted to tell me last night—with his wife listening in! Do you believe that! You can bet I wasn't pleased sharing a conversation. Men! Sometimes I wonder why we women bother. They can be so stupid."

“He what?” Jenny was aghast. “I’ll make myself scarce when he calls. Just tell me afterwards, please.”

“I’ll share what you need to know, sweetie. Anyhow, I have to get out of these things and into sweats and a T. Then I’ll start dinner. I’ll make a frittata after I’ve heard from Brad. Won’t take long if I prep it now. While I’m doing that, you can tell me about your day.”

That’s one thing I love about my mom, Jenny thought. *Doesn’t matter what happens. Life goes on. Hope I’m like that when I’m her age.*

Chapter 40
Reporting and Reflecting

4:45 p.m., Tuesday, October 27th
Phone from Brad's car, Montreal, to West Condos, Halifax

Brad parked his car on the lakefront in Pointe Claire and speed-dialed Kate's number. She answered immediately. "Where are you?"

"Don't worry," he said. "I'm in the car. And Jill's not here. Sorry about that, Kate. Dumb idea."

"Tell me what happened."

He had to be honest, no matter the consequences. "Jill wants to try again, but I'm insisting that it's over. She says she can change and that I can, too. She seems to mean it. But I know her, and even if I didn't have you, I don't think we could make one another happy."

"So, what did you tell her?"

"I talked separation. She knows about you, but not much beyond your name and that you're in Halifax. She knows I've been seeing you, though she's not certain for how long, even though I told her we only met last weekend."

"That's probably information she can take to a lawyer when it gets down to that. Is it going that route, Brad? Are you and Jill really over?"

"She's trying hard to entice me back, but I'm making it clear I've lost interest. It is over, but she won't accept it. Until she does, we can't discuss the how and the when and who gets what and the place for the boys."

Kate was silent. Brad heard the hesitation in her voice when she spoke. "Have you told her about the possibility of a move here to work? That would shake her up, I bet. That and if you start talking legal separation. Seems to me she thinks she can keep talking about resurrecting your dead marriage for months."

He thought it strange Kate was seeking a quick resolution of his divorce, considering her own divorce was still wending its way through the lawyers' offices and courts. Nevertheless, he agreed with her suggestions. "When I get home and we get down to talking again, I'll put that word 'legal' in front of separation every time. And I'll pick a time to announce the probable relocation."

"Probable?" Kate asked.

"I don't want her thinking that I want to go. Better that I say I'm being pressured to take over the Halifax office, otherwise she'll think you and I have manipulated the offer. I have to play this card carefully. It's a key."

"I suppose so, but play it soon, please," Kate said.

"I will, but we have to keep in mind that we can't rush this. It will take time. A lot more than the five days we've known one another. That we've come this far in such a short time is a miracle of love. Whoops! There goes that word again!" Brad laughed, trying to lighten the moment.

Kate seemed determined to keep things moving. "What's the immediate plan?"

"I'll start talking legal separation. I'll draw up a 'separation to do' list and share it with her and look for a chance to mention the board urging me to take over the Maritime branch. And I will continue to sleep in the spare room, resisting Jill's attempts to seduce me."

"Oh, you didn't mention that."

He didn't know whether she was serious or joking. "Well, I did say she was trying to entice me back into our marriage. The other thing is that she's being so agreeable. It's almost like this isn't the real Jill."

"Just keep saying no, Brad. And what do you mean 'not the real Jill'?"

"Oh, just that she should be angry at me wanting out. But she isn't. Or she's pretending not to be. That's not Jill. Almost as if she can seduce me and then I'll cave."

"Obviously I don't know her, but it sounds like she has a plan. Don't you dare cave in. Do you have a lawyer? Is it time to talk to one?"

"I have the lawyer recommended by her father. We used him for the house purchase, but I don't think I should use him. I have a long-time friend I can talk to. I'll do that at work tomorrow."

"Sounds better to get your friend than someone Jill knows."

"You're probably right." After an unusual silence, he continued, "Well, I have to get home. Jill's expecting me, and we're scheduled to do more talking. I think I'll try to speak to the boys separately. Together, Jill uses them as levers to get me back in line. Her line, that is."

"I'm working days until Saturday, and then I have four days off before I start nights next Thursday. I'm impossible and totally unreasonable when I'm on nights, so call me before they start."

"You do have a dark side, then," Brad teased. "I will call you Friday at the latest. Earlier if there's any progress, any movement, any change—good or bad."

"It had better be good news or you *will* see my dark side. Even though I love you, Mr. Anderson, I have to cultivate my dark side in case true love doesn't run smoothly."

He laughed again and responded, “I’ll have to make sure I keep you happy, then. Bye, Kate. Say hello to Jenny.”

“Bye, Brad. Say goodbye to Jill,” and she hung up before he could reply.

* * *

Kate thought Brad was right. After five days, she was insane to expect things to move quickly. It had been almost two years since she and Mike had begun divorce proceedings, and it still wasn’t final. But she was crazy over this new love, and patience was not an ally to craziness. Just as she was convincing herself to slow down, her daughter emerged from the room to which she’d discretely vanished when Brad called.

“Anything new and exciting?” Jenny asked, adding, “That you can share.”

Kate gave her the important news and accompanied it with her realization that she was over-expecting and had to learn patience. She even asked her daughter if she thought her mother was crazy to expect this much from a liaison that only dated back five days.

Jenny hugged her and reassured her, telling of the changes she’d seen in her mother over the weekend. Good changes. She then told Kate that it was sixteen-year-olds who were impatient and demanding and hormonal when they had never-to-be-ended crushes. She would try to ensure her middle-aged mother did not behave that way and would be her understanding, patient, tolerant, restraining support. She would make sure her mother did her homework and kept to a curfew and . . .

Her daughter would have continued except Kate pretend-smothered her with a cushion before announcing that supper included a broccoli salad and Jenny would be expected to eat her greens, precocious child that she was.

* * *

Brad didn’t want his sons in the conversation he needed to have with Jill. She knew he wanted out, and the only discussion should be about the particulars of the living and parenting arrangements. He had to get her to agree it was over, and if the boys were present, she’d use them to engender guilt in him. Goodness knows the only guilt he experienced in this whole shemozzle was what this would do to the boys, especially James. He didn’t need Jill turning the thumbscrews.

He took out his tablet and his list of what had to be decided when they separated. Then, almost as if his resolve might fail in front of her, he made another list to remind him what he had to tell her.

He called to suggest they meet first before talking with the boys, and she was far from pleased when he asked if they could meet in her office at the real estate company in Pointe Claire.

"There's lasagna in the oven, and not a store-bought one. I've been looking forward to dinner."

"Oh, cut out the blackmail and the seduction, Jill," he barked into his phone. "I want out. Our marriage can't be fixed. Let's agree on that and then talk to the boys about possibilities. I can't come home and play happy families any more. Let's deal with it."

"Fine. I'll feed the boys and explain that you won't be joining us for dinner." Her voice was restrained, and he realized the boys were hearing her hurt response.

"I'll meet you at the office in forty-five minutes," he said. They had to get this over with. To hell with Jill and her games.

Chapter 41
Leaving and Leftovers

7:00 p.m., Tuesday, October 27th
Treetops Terrace, Kirkland, Montreal

Harry's eyes widened when his mother entered the dining room, where he waited for his brother to finish the lasagna he was pushing around the plate.

"Are you sure you're going to meet Dad? That's more like the"—he hesitated rather than employ the vernacular—"sort of clothing you'd wear to meet the 'A' guy."

He knew his parents were trying to sort out their situation without him and James knowing all the details. He also realized they didn't want him, and especially his much more sensitive brother, to witness explosive arguments. Perhaps that's what his father was trying to avoid. But why would his mother be dressed like a . . . a—there wasn't a "motherly" word he could apply to his mother, tarted up the way she was. He wasn't sure what was going on.

When she bent to hug James, a tear drifted down James' cheek. The quiet plea seemed to follow it into the half-eaten plate of lasagna and Harry barely heard, "Do you have to go? If Dad was here, you could sort things out. Where is he? Where are you going?"

Harry wasn't sure whether the hug became tighter or whether his mother tensed to prevent her own tears. She reassured James that she and his father would be home before nine and might even be earlier. Maybe that made his brother feel better, but it didn't help Harry's attitude.

When James squirmed from her arms and raced out of the room, she snatched her purse, donned her matching jacket, and with a last check of her face in the dining room mirror, headed to the front door.

Harry watched her movements with interest. He would try to explain to his brother things he barely understood. But first, he had to clean up the lasagna James quite deliberately dropped on the floor before running upstairs.

* * *

James tried to slam his bedroom door, but it didn't make much noise until, with both hands in front of him, he body-checked it. Still, it didn't sound as loud as he'd wanted. And what difference? His parents weren't there to hear it.

He was so angry that he was crying, which didn't make sense. He picked up his action figures that were displayed on two shelves and, one by one, threw them at the door and walls. The closed blinds saved the windows. Sobbing uncontrollably, he fell to the bed and clutched his beat-up He-Haw as hard as he could.

He heard Harry come up the stairs and stop at the door. James wanted to apologize about the lasagna mess. He wanted his big brother, who understood everything, to hug him.

The door cracked open. "Who are we giving your leftovers to? Mom or Dad?" Harry snickered. "They'll never know it was on the floor."

James dried his tears and grinned. "Maybe they'll have eaten out. Or was there some left in the dish?"

"There's lots left, but I can serve them what you threw on the floor if you want."

* * *

As James' anger diminished, Harry asked what he wanted to know. "Can't promise I have all the answers, but ask away."

"What's going to happen to us?"

"Whoa! Start with the easy ones, please." Harry grinned though he didn't really feel like it. But he had to cheer up his brother.

"Do you think Mom and Dad will stay together?" James asked.

"I think that's what they're talking about right now," Harry said. "Mom didn't want to at first cos she met someone else. Now she wants Dad, but he doesn't seem happy being with her. Maybe we'll know more about that when they get back home."

"Are we going to have to move? Who do we live with? Dad or Mom? But you won't be here, will you? You're off to college soon. Who will I talk to when you're gone? Sometimes I think you're the only one in this family who cares."

Harry sensed the anxiety in his brother's voice. "Slow down, kiddo. Mom and Dad both love you. It's just they're so wrapped up in their difficulties that you think they're neglecting you. But when it comes to the crunch, they'll be fighting about who can look after you best. That is, if they do separate. Let's wait and see what happens when they come back. I have homework to do." He hoped James didn't see through his lie. "Talk to you later, okay?" He tousled his brother's hair before leaving.

In his room, Harry removed the rolled socks from his drawer, extracted a joint, and sneaked to the deck, where he lit up and inhaled the harsh, but immediately relaxing, smoke.

Chapter 42
Thrusts and Threats

7:30 p.m., Tuesday, October 27th
West Isle Real Estate, Pointe Claire, Montreal

Brad parked his car beside his wife's. The security guard let them into the seemingly deserted building when Jill, whom the guard knew, said she and her client had papers to verify.

Once in the office, with Jill behind the desk and Brad sunk into an armchair, the conversation began.

Difficult as it must have been, Jill spoke first. It seemed she was ready to turn on her charms at the first sign of a positive response from him, as though she believed that if she seduced him, she could make him hers once more. Her body language suggested she had more to offer sexually than Kate did, not to mention that outfit.

"How was Kate when you spoke to her? I assume you've brought her up to date. I hope she's forgiven you for last night's mistake. No, that's a lie! I hope she never forgives you."

"I spoke to her about an hour ago. Told her I was determined to separate from you, and once that was arranged, she and I could plan our future."

Jill's facade of understanding and accord slipped after his response. "That's a bit premature, isn't it?" Her speech was less measured though he detected anxiety in the tone. "You know we can still make a go of this. We can change the things that we now know annoy each other."

Desperation had crept in. He sensed his wife's conciliatory approach was weakening.

"If we try and it doesn't work out, then you can seek out Kate. Surely she'll understand." Another pause. "Is she a mother, Brad? If she is, she must know we have a responsibility to Harry and James."

She rose from her chair and moved from behind the desk to sit in the other armchair closer to him, curling her long legs under her to reveal their full and provocative length, topped by a skirt that hid little but promised much.

The move only angered him. He hauled himself out of the chair to perch on a corner of the desk above her. "Cut it out, Jill. Your seduction techniques may have helped you sell to others in this office, but I am not in the market. What part of 'I want out' do you not understand? It's over between us. Just like you found Aaron, I've found somebody else."

Jill sprang from her seat, switching from passive seductive to near aggression. "I'm through with Aaron, so forget that justification for you and Kate. It's you I want. I know I've been a selfish cow, but you must know how easy it is to wander, especially when you don't think you're loved at home? I—"

"You're wasting your time, Jill. What we need to do now is plan how we can legally separate with minimal hurt to the boys." He wanted to push home the advantage he was gaining. "I have a list. We can make copies if I can transfer it to the computer here. It's what I thought we should do once we get a legal separation. We can take our time and get it right if we follow my list—that is, if you agree with it. Here, read it."

He passed his tablet to her. She brushed his arm aside and unfolded herself to stand, face to face with him. Her agreeable front had been abandoned. It was fight time.

"There had to be a list, didn't there, Brad? You have an effing list for everything. Do you give Kate a list before you screw her? Have you got lists for Harry and James in there? I don't want your stupid list. I don't want a legal separation. I want you, Brad. Though right now I don't know why. You are the most frustrating man I have ever known. I thought you didn't have a spontaneous bone in your body, but you must have if you got it on with Kate. Or maybe she was on one of your lists. Maybe the one that says, 'Women I Can Have an Affair with to Piss Off Jill'."

Brad rose from the desk, pushed past her, and ambled toward the office door. It was locked.

Jill dangled the key in her outstretched hand and continued her tirade. "I hope you're on your way to find a lawyer because you're going to need one."

He wasn't sure whether he'd won, and if he had, what would be the cost of the victory?

* * *

Jill didn't know whether to scream more threats or dissolve into tears, not that she could control either choice. She was letting out her frustrations and the target, the man she thought she still loved, was in front of her, holding out his hand and asking for the key. There was no way she'd let him escape until she finished.

"Legal separation," she screamed. "A list for legal separation. Then divorce. Well, both need lawyers, and I'm using Dad's so you can find another. And good luck with that because I intend dragging you and this Kate bitch through the dirt of court hearings. I'm getting the house. And you won't get near James if I have anything to do with it, and kiss your expensive habits goodbye because I'm getting what's mine."

Brad said nothing, probably because she wouldn't shut up. Then she made the mistake of pausing to breathe as tears slid down her cheeks. Sobs emerged in place of the angry words that had flowed freely seconds previously. She felt small and vulnerable. If only Brad would say what she wanted to hear. But that wouldn't happen.

True to form, he responded, "It's all on the list, Jill."

"That fucking list! I hate your lists, and I hate this one most of all. Show it to your lawyer because we're through. There! You've got what you wanted."

She threw the keys at him and watched him duck when they flew by his head. When he bent to retrieve them, he said, "There's one thing I didn't put on the list. You might as well hear it now. I have the opportunity to take over the company's Halifax office and move there. Kate likes that idea."

"I bet she does! And how long has all this been going on? Before I hooked up with Aaron? How long?" She tried to hold back her tears.

He turned and displayed that annoying smile. "I just met her last Thursday. About five days ago, almost to the minute."

Jill was astounded. The room was the quietest it had been since they entered. "You have to be kidding me. Not even a week? You mean all this divorce talk and moving to Halifax is over someone you met just days ago? Jesus, Brad. You're on a schoolboy crush. Some fresh piece has let you have it and you're besotted. Give me that key, and call me when it's over. I'll be home later. Tell the boys we're through—for now—until you come to your senses. Just let me know what you tell them. I know! Leave me a list!"

* * *

Jill unlocked the door and flounced down the hallway. Brad heard her piercing voice asking security to lock up when her client left.

He straightened the desk, the sort of thing he resorted to when he was upset. Order gave him comfort, just like making "to do" lists when faced with a major crisis. Jill understood that, and he didn't understand how his lists could make her so angry.

What about her final tirade? No, not the one about talking to the boys; he'd make a list of what to tell them when he got in the car. The comment about him having a schoolboy crush on Kate was the one that jolted him. Jill couldn't be right about that, could she?"

He turned off the lights, said a curt goodnight when he passed the stern security guard, and ambled toward his car. Jill's was long gone. He inserted the key, deciding he didn't need a list to prompt what he'd say to his sons. He hoped Jill's hurried departure didn't mean she'd get home first before he had a chance to tell his version of events.

He quickly sped along the TransCanada to the Chemin Ste. Marie exit, anxious to find out.

Chapter 43
Plus Ça Change, Plus C'est la Même Chose

9:00 p.m., Tuesday, October 27th
Phone from Lakeside Condos to a bar in one of the West Island Holiday Inns

Aaron's least favourite nights were Mondays and Tuesdays. He called them his recovery nights. After the weekends, not much action existed anywhere. For that, he was sometimes grateful because he needed rest after the weekend's exertions. The past weekend was no exception after he'd hooked up with Sophia, who followed a little too closely on the heels of Jill.

Monday after work, he had slept and replenished. This evening would be conducive to maintaining or renewing contacts. Phone, text, tweet, IM—all available to help in the search. He'd even made a couple of satisfying contacts that had begun on Facebook. Occasionally, he scouted what he called the "desperately available lists" on line.

His thoughts turned back to Jill. Maybe she was having fond memories of him.

He'd called Chrissie earlier, who'd said that Jill was almost certainly splitting from her husband. Perhaps, he speculated, it was time to see if she would accept the occasional liaison with him. She could only say no.

He found her on speed dial. If she picked up after recognising his number, he had a chance.

* * *

The large glass of red wine was almost gone, and Jill debated whether to go home, mend fences, and offer comfort to her kids or have a second Merlot. If she stayed at this hotel bar, a businessman in town for meetings or a guy not wanting to go home to an unwelcoming abode would hit on her. It was not surprising she was receiving looks of appraisal. She'd dolled herself up for Brad. That was a laugh! Before she could decide whether to order another glass or go home to pick up pieces of a failing marriage, her phone buzzed.

She assumed it would be Brad or one of the boys and was surprised to see Aaron's number. She stopped and considered her options for three seconds before issuing a welcome and saying, "What a delightful surprise."

What seeds had Chrissie sown, Jill wondered, when Aaron told her that her friend had spilled the beans about her impending marriage breakup. She told him she was having a calm-down drink after another fight with Brad and relayed where she was. "Want to join me while I drown my sorrows?" She hastily added that, after the evening's revelations, she was not sorry to see Brad depart.

She was more than disappointed when Aaron declined her invitation. No doubt a made-up excuse. He must still have that young student hanging around. But why call her?

And then her mood changed for the better when he invited her to lunch the following day, at a restaurant they had enjoyed and frequented the past six months. She didn't hesitate to accept, adding that she had always liked lunch there because it often preceded afternoon delight at his place or at one of the empty condos he was trying to sell.

Aaron laughed. "The best ones were the furnished ones. They, at least, had beds."

She had better finish this risqué conversation. Other than the occasional lunch, she might want to cease further involvement with Aaron. Depending upon what happened at home.

"I'm about to be hit on if I stay here any longer, and I don't mean by you. I'll see you tomorrow at 12:30. Looking forward to it!" Lunch would be the time to discover Aaron's true intentions.

Jill finished the call, paid the bill, and drove slowly along the service road. What waited at home? Halfway there, she realized it was well past the nine o'clock deadline she'd promised James.

* * *

A sibilant "Yesss!" came from Aaron after Jill hung up. He wondered whether it would be safe to bring Jill back to his place the next afternoon. She would accept the comfort he wanted to bestow upon her. If she didn't want to risk her car being spotted, they could check out those new condos in Lachine. He could get the keys from his agent friend, who would know the last thing they needed was a guide.

On impulse he phoned Chrissie. "Guess who I just spoke to?"

"You didn't call Jill, did you, you callous bastard?"

"And who's having lunch with me tomorrow? And who may want to explore the delights of some new condos after?"

“Aaron, hold on. I thought she was trying to save her marriage. Has something happened?”

“Not so. I think they’ve had a major blow up because Jill was in a bar drowning her sorrows. Or maybe celebrating. Not sure which. I’ll tell you which after tomorrow.”

Chrissie uttered words of caution. “If they’ve split for good, Jill will be very vulnerable—”

“That’s what I’m hoping for.” He couldn’t wait.

“Be gentle with her. She needs more than the consolation I’m sure you plan to give her. Who knows, Aaron, this might be a ploy to move in with you,” Chrissie said.

Chrissie hung up before he had chance to consider that possibility.

Chapter 44
Missing and Misgivings

9:45 p.m., Tuesday, October 27th
Treetops Terrace, Kirkland, Montreal

"It's gone to voicemail again," Brad told his two sons. "I bet she's driving home and can't pick up." He noticed the look on Harry's face and added, "I'm sure she'll be here any minute."

Almost an hour previously, when Brad walked into the house, he discovered he had his sons to himself. Two anxious teens waited for a satisfying explanation of their future. At first, he thought he had an opportunity to explain his side of the story, free from Jill's interruptions and sarcasm, but he quickly realized both boys were watching for their mother to come through the door. His attempts to explain what might happen needed Jill's affirmation or contradiction before the boys would accept words from him.

As gently as he possibly could, with both boys across from him at the dining room table, he explained he and their mother would be separating, that they were too unhappy to live together any more. "We fight too much, and I'm sure our unhappiness makes both of you unhappy."

"You got that right," Harry blurted. "But I need to hear what Mom says about this. What's going to happen to us? Where will we live? Who will we live with? Can we stay here with our friends and go to the same school?"

James reached for Harry's hand resting on the table. Brad leaned forward to emphasize his concern. "These are details your mom and I still have to work out, and we will do that with your help and taking your ideas into consideration."

It again hit Brad that his wife was much better talking to the boys than he was. He struggled to reach them, a fact emphasized when James said, "I think you and Mom should try harder. Can't you get help to stay together?"

Harry answered that question with, "Sorry, James, but I think Dad's given up trying and maybe Mom, too, if she ever gets here to let us know."

* * *

James wanted his mother. His father had returned home from another trip away and suddenly everything changed. He was supposed to come home and sort things out; he promised to do that. He even came home on the Sunday after James phoned to ask him to come home. But now he was saying their marriage couldn't be fixed.

James needed to ask Harry questions but didn't want his dad to hear. "Can Harry and I have a talk?" he asked his father.

"You can ask whatever you want," his father replied, looking surprised at his request.

"Harry can help me, and I don't want you to hear."

His father frowned.

Was he upset?

"Just one more thing I should tell you." His father's words seemed scratchy, as if they stuck in his throat. "I may be starting a new job that will take me away from here next year. I could be going to Halifax in May. That's a couple of months before you start at Dalhousie, Harry."

"Oh fuck, Dad! Why the fuck do you think I wanted to go away to college? I could have gone to McGill or Concordia, but I needed to get away from you and Mom. I need to escape from this goddamn bickering, somewhere I don't hear it every fucking day. Mom's right! It's you that wants to break up this family. You've got someone else so you don't understand any fucking thing."

James knew his big brother swore with his friends, but he'd never heard him go off at their father. He glanced at his father, waiting for him to punish Harry for swearing and condemn his attitude. His father's head remained bowed, though, staring at his tablet. He had a list on it and had referred to it while talking to them.

"Come on, James," Harry said. "Come up to my room until Mom gets home. I'll try to answer your questions, but they're probably the same ones I have."

James had his big brother on his side. Harry must want to help him since he'd invited him into his room. First time ever.

* * *

Not only was Brad inept at engaging his boys in a serious conversation, but he knew Jill was aware of that. She was probably staying out, knowing he was doing more harm to himself than good. It was her turn to return to the scene and play the upset, helpless saviour who rescued the day.

Everything had gone wrong. Trouble was, when Jill did appear, she would turn the screw and manipulate the boys' mistrust of him and round two would be hers. As a bonus, he'd probably given enough ammunition for succeeding rounds. Boy, had he blown this one.

While he was trying to calculate the questions James would have for Harry and realized he could no longer think like a teen, headlights swept across the drapes when Jill's car turned in the driveway.

Brad quickly tried to devise a strategy for the upcoming situation. But when the boys' footsteps pounded down the stairs, he acknowledged he was in a defensive position and would have to respond carefully to Jill's cunning and probably underhanded attacks.

Chapter 45
Attack and Defence

10:00 p.m., Tuesday, October 23rd
Treetops Terrace, Kirkland, Montreal

"That'll be Mom," Harry told James when headlights swept the walls of his dimly lit room. Silently, he thanked his mother for arriving to save him from questions to which he had no answers. Hard to believe he had the same questions as his kid brother.

"Come on, James. Maybe Mom can tell us what's going to happen."

Downstairs, Harry stood back to let James hug their mom as soon as she came through the door. Their father was still at the table, typing into the ever-present tablet. *Bet it's another list.*

His mother echoed his thoughts when she greeted her husband. "Another list, Brad?"

"No, just notes to prevent me from saying the wrong thing. I've done that enough already tonight."

Harry thought that statement, though true, would encourage his mother to criticize his father. He didn't quite know why, but he tried to delay the attack. He helped his mother toward her favourite armchair, sat on the arm of it, and told her that his father had told him and James that the marriage was over. "We need to know what's going to happen, Mom. Where will we all live?"

His mother beckoned James to sit on the rug by her feet. She spoke slowly. "Yes, Harry, and you, James, that's what we decided. That's what your father wanted. What else did you tell them, Brad?"

The situation was almost like a video game attack, Harry thought, recognising the feint that preceded the proper onslaught. His father was slumped on the sofa. Harry thought his father had avoided the invitation to dig himself into a deeper hole when he said, "No, Jill, I think we both agreed that separation was inevitable."

James' small voice from the floor said, "What's 'inevitable' mean, Mom?"

Harry beat his mother to the answer though she would have said something similar. "It means something has to happen!" Harry presented his palm to his mother for a high five and quickly dropped it.

James peered at his mother. "And does it have to happen, Mom?"

Way to go, Harry thought. *One question from little brother and the battle starts again.*

* * *

Jill still wasn't sure what had gone on between the boys and her strangely quiet husband. The boys' body language alone indicated that what they'd heard hadn't endeared their father to them. She spotted her opportunity and jumped in. "I'm not one hundred percent sure that separation and divorce has to happen," she said, ruffling James' hair while bringing the "D" word into the equation. "I hoped we could start again, but your dad thinks it's too late."

Brad jumped in, but he was already coming from a losing position, and his first words didn't help. "Yes, that's true, but—"

She seized another moment. "But what, Brad? But you think it's too late, or you don't want to try anymore?"

Brad looked at his page of notes as though searching for an answer.

"And what else did Dad tell you, James?" she asked.

That quiet, but surprisingly decisive voice came before Harry could intervene. James said, "He's moving to Halifax next year."

"That went down real well," her older son added. "I was hoping to escape parent problems by going there to school. Now what?"

When Brad eased forward in the sofa, with his notebook resting on the arm—two signs Jill recognized as preliminaries to a speech—she cut him off before he started. "And did your father tell you more about the girlfriend he has in Halifax?"

A stunned pause ensued before three voices spoke simultaneously. James' simple "No" and Harry's "OMG, it all makes sense now!" were drowned out by "Jesus, Jill, that's not fair. That's separate from us breaking up. I told you that. Anyhow, what about Aaron?"

She had advanced beyond the opening salvos. Both boys were on her side. And almost every time Brad opened his mouth, more ammunition spewed for the lawyer she was going to seek the following day. Brad had brought the topic up, so a little twisting of the truth wouldn't hurt. "I told you and the boys that Aaron had finished with me."

Brad ignored her and appealed to his sons. "It's not exactly like your mom is telling it. Halifax has nothing to do with—" He stood and hovered over the family group clustered around the armchair. "Jill! Boys! I can't do this. It's too late, and facts are getting twisted, and you boys are beginning to hate me. We need to talk again, maybe tomorrow evening. Just know this. I love you both, and I don't want to hurt you."

What was coming next? Was he really giving up on the night's battle? Her answer came when Brad asked James if he could "borrow" her for a moment. "Let go of her legs, son."

She shrugged. "Okay, boys, why don't you go to your rooms. Either your dad or I will be up to talk later. If you're still awake."

* * *

When Brad heard both bedroom doors close, he told Jill what he'd decided. "This is as good a time as any to make a break."

"What do you mean? We still have lots to talk about. We can fix this if we both try."

"You don't get it, do you, Jill. Or maybe you do and you're playing for a new future. I don't want to try anymore. For me, it's over. For me, we can't sort out the details without help. We both need to see a lawyer—and soon—because I'm gone!"

"Where to? Are you moving out?"

"Just temporarily," he said. "I'll be in touch after work tomorrow when I'm less confused. Right now, I can only think of packing a bag and finding a hotel. Tell the boys whatever you want, but tell them I'll call tomorrow."

* * *

Jill watched her husband trudge up the stairs. She resisted the urge to follow. It would be too much sarcasm to ask if he needed help packing a bag. She sank into the comfort and consolation of the armchair, wrapping her arms around herself.

The silence was only broken by the muffled sound of Harry's music until Brad reappeared carrying a tote. She wondered how they'd say goodbye in such a situation.

He stopped at the foot of the stairs and set down the bag. She first assumed he was inviting a farewell hug and inappropriate words of comfort. Instead he rummaged in the hall closet.

He then turned toward her. Again, she wondered about goodbye words.

The ever-practical Brad did not disappoint. "I left a credit card on your dresser. Don't go crazy, but use it for whatever you and the boys need until we sort things out. I'm sorry it has to be this way, but we'll pick up the pieces and survive."

She tried to haul herself out of the chair. Brad deserved a hug for that speech and for the hatchet job she'd done on him earlier. She needed one, too. But before she was upright, the door had slammed behind him.

He had gone.

She sat again, vainly trying to disappear within herself when the tears flowed and her body heaved with sobs. The boys deserved an explanation, and she promised herself she would put the hatchet away and present a fair picture of Brad's departure to Harry and James.

As she calmed down, she had a passing thought. Brad had walked out on her. Rule one of divorce: He/she who walks away loses.

Tears streamed again. "Oh, the foolish man," she muttered.

Her strange sadness was interrupted by James' voice from the stairs. "When are you coming up, Mom?"

Chapter 46
Five Days. A Lifetime

Midnight, Tuesday, October 27th
Quality Suites, Boulevard Hymus, Pointe Claire, Montreal

Brad still had his phone in his hand even though he'd decided, ten minutes previously, that to phone Kate would be a dumb idea. She'd be in bed and set to get up early for work. But, other than disturbing her sleep, what good would it do? His emotions were all over the place, and he doubted his thought processes were working right. God knows he'd already made enough mistakes and misjudgments for one day. And it would be a good news/bad news situation he'd be reporting.

Kate might be pleased he'd made the break, but she wouldn't be pleased he'd walked out—abandoning his wife and sons. At least that's the way the courts would see it. And Jill was getting a lawyer the next day. She knew Kate's name and that it had been a five-day romance. She also knew the Halifax job was a possibility—if the divorce didn't scupper it. Harry might change his mind about going to Dalhousie. Somehow, Brad had managed to turn both boys away from him and to Jill's side.

The news could wait until the following day, after Kate was finished work. There was more bad than good news, and she might not want to hear any of it.

He could do with a drink, but he'd chosen the wrong hotel. No lounge. No mini-bar.

Sleep was impossible, and the next day seemed likely to be as bad as the day he'd just endured. Five days previously he'd flown into Halifax. Who would have believed what those five days would have brought.

* * *

Jill managed to contain her grief when she comforted James, and she stayed with him until he was almost asleep. She thought she had been honest with her answers. Had her anger been foremost, she could have turned her youngest against his father. But the upset at the whole mishmash that wasn't, in her mind, a true separation prevented her from slanging her husband. Or was he now her ex?

The day had turned into such a mess, but Jill was convinced she could make the changes necessary to salvage and regrow their marriage. It was clear that Brad couldn't, and wouldn't, make the effort.

She lay, fully clothed, on her bed. James was asleep, probably a restless sleep. Faint music still came from Harry's room. Jill wondered if he wanted to talk, but she wouldn't know where to start with him. She was afraid Harry's anger at his father might trigger hers. Difficult as it was, she had to keep a clear head.

She almost laughed out loud. Clear-headed Jill. That was a rare species. She was emotion and reaction, impulse and opportunity. But her lawyer wouldn't see that side of her. She hoped she could arrange a meeting in the morning. She should make a list of things she needed to share with her lawyer. She chuckled. Lists were Brad's prerogative. She was better than her husband when it came to thinking on one's feet. Even though he wouldn't be there in the morning, she'd spin the tale of events in her favour.

Still fully dressed, she fell into a fitful sleep with Harry's music offering escape and comfort only to him.

* * *

Kate gave up trying to sleep. Past midnight. She would be sleep-walking through her shift in the morning. She switched on the bedside light and sipped from the glass of warm water on the bedside table. She checked her phone to make sure she hadn't missed a text or a call from Brad.

Nothing, which was why she was still awake. She wanted news! She needed news! Her life was in limbo. She wanted good news, but if what Brad had to tell her wasn't what she wanted to hear, she could move on. Could Brad be permanent? She wanted to know what had happened, and for an instant considered calling him.

It wasn't common sense or self-control that stopped her. She recalled a woman she had worked with who had enjoyed a series of inconsequential sexual relationships after her divorce. They became known as "shits that pass in the night." And maybe that's all Brad was. She doubted it, but maybe her judgement of this man was naive.

On her way back to her room from a bathroom visit, she quietly opened Jenny's door. At sixteen, one could sleep anywhere, anytime, forever. Kate wondered at what age that luxury was interfered with by life's demands and anxiety-induced thoughts.

She turned off the light and assumed the position that usually led to sleep. Maybe Brad would call before she left for work in the morning.

Her last thought was that Jill might be as awake and uncertain as she was. Or maybe Jill was snuggled up with Brad.

Part Three

CONSIDERATIONS

Love.
Partaking of this drug causes false thinking
and actions worse than rum-sodden behaviours.
The effects last much longer
and leave a hangover for which marriage,
perhaps,
is the most popular cure.

Chapter 47
Aaron's Options

Late afternoon, Friday, November 27th
Lakeside Condominiums, Pointe Claire, PQ

The sun was setting behind the thin cloud to the southwest, across lac St. Louis. Not bad weather for a Friday in late November. No signs of snow though the days were getting shorter.

Aaron observed that it might not be a bad evening for barhopping, either on the Plateau or even downtown. That was choice number four. Chrissie was seeking a pre-Christmas party they could crash, but late November was not a popular party time, and she was not optimistic. He had calls in to Jill and to Sophia, hoping one of them would disturb his reverie while he rested for the weekend's social activities.

He sensed Sophia was avoiding him. Her enthusiasm and availability had diminished since the student party she had dragged him to. He had felt out of place and had not endeared himself to the sulking Sophia when he insisted they leave and drive to his apartment. She'd seemed more interested in one of her contemporaries, who was all over her. If she didn't respond to his text this time, he would cross her off his list. Perhaps she was too young to appreciate all he had to offer.

In contrast, Jill seemed to be available whenever he called. He did not call so frequently that she might think he sought more than occasional meetings. Their get-togethers were mostly for drinks, coffee, or lunch; however, in the month since Aaron found out Jill's husband had walked out on her and the boys, she had finished up in Aaron's bed on more than one occasion. The old enthusiasm and enjoyment were still evident, though the first time they surrendered to their former passion she had cried.

He had avoided getting involved in Jill's marital situation or even discussing it. He saw himself as offering her an escape from its stresses. Chrissie had told him that initial separation negotiations were already bitter. He was quite happy if Jill simply wanted to use him. There had been no more talk of permanence, and she seemed to be much more discrete and secretive in arranging their assignations.

He was dozing when his phone chirped. It was Jill with an invitation to dinner at her place. Just the two of them. For a moment, the invitation worried him. What had happened to secrecy? Was this an introduction to her changed prospects of domesticity? Then she explained that Brad and the boys were on the 5:30 p.m. flight for a weekend in Halifax to meet Brad's paramour.

"I can escape with a bottle or three of wine, but I'd much prefer you distract me," she said.

There was something perverse that led Jill to invite him for a weekend rendezvous at the family home. This would be a first. Cautiously, he asked, "Are you sure of this, Jill?"

"It's what I need. It's what I want, and yes, I am sure."

He was about to suggest he bring a weekend bag when Jill continued, "And don't read anything into this, Aaron. This is revenge and this is escape. I'm all over the place emotionally. You may not want to get too comfortable. You may find yourself dining with a bitch."

He set aside thoughts of a weekend stay. The event could be momentous, or it could end before it even began. He played it casually. "Understood, I think. What time for dinner, and can I bring anything?"

"About eight. But get here whenever you want to, and you know what you have that I need." With a throaty chuckle, she cut him off.

For the first time, he wondered if he was taking unfair advantage of this hurting and recovering woman. But she was making all the overtures. She was using him, which was a novelty for someone who had, for years, seen himself as the user, enjoying such a status. Was that all there was to him? Were all his intimate relationships based solely on that role?

He hoped not.

As he showered and changed, Aaron told himself to treat Jill with respect and tenderness. After all, he was being invited to share more than her bed. And all this while her husband was sharing a domestic experience with his new woman.

The situation needed careful consideration. Briefly, he questioned his new approach to this date. Was he looking beyond a sexual liaison? Was he in danger of becoming further involved in Jill's split from Brad? And did Jill need him for anything other than a physical panacea for Brad's transfer of affection?

He settled for Jill needing him, but as insurance, he'd call Chrissie and get her take on this new development.

Chapter 48
The Boys' Road Trip

5:50 p.m., Friday, November 27th
En route to Halifax International from P.E.T. Airport, Montreal

Harry looked across the aisle of the Bombardier airbus in time to see James remove his hand from their father's grasp. The plane had broken through the clouds and was heading east into the darkening skies. The woman in the seat next to Harry was already engrossed in a book whose title Harry could not discern. It might be a short but quiet flight.

His father interrupted his thoughts. "You okay by yourself, or do you want to sit with James?"

"I'm good," he replied. "I might try to have a nap. You can keep James amused, Dad."

Again, Harry wanted to make sense of what was happening to his family. A number of restless nights had failed to provide a satisfying answer. His dad's midweek announcement that he was taking his sons to an ocean resort near Halifax fitted somewhere into the family equation, especially after the throwaway remark that Harry and James would get to meet Kate and her daughter, Jenny.

Harry pushed his seat back, closed his eyes, and pretended to doze. In fact, his mind worked overtime. Neither of his parents knew he had already made online contact with Jenny. They texted regularly after a couple of FaceTime sessions, when both gave perceptions of their parents' expectations in their new relationships. He quickly discovered that Jenny's mother wanted far more than a Maritime affair. He had told Jenny that his father was finished with his mother even though she wanted to save the marriage. She was upset at the separation and was still inclined to fight it. Jenny told him she didn't know whether she was pleased or scared that lawyers were involved, and she had confided that she hoped things between their parents could be resolved without too much hurt.

Texts at the airport had confirmed that Jenny looked forward to getting to know him. He felt the same way. While FaceTime and selfies were never the most flattering, Jenny looked attractive. Their online conversations and texts had, unbeknownst to their parents, established a union intent upon helping Brad and Kate.

As Harry tried to relax, the unanswerable question kept recurring. If Kate and his dad became a permanent item, how could his mother be happy? More questions followed. Though his father had told him about Kate, what if she turned out to be a manipulative bitch who was fooling his father? Where would Harry's allegiance lie? Was it possible to be supportive of both parents when each went in a different direction? How the hell could he do that? Would he even like this Kate woman? And where would he go to school next year? So many questions and so few answers. And even more decisions impossible to make.

While he pondered whether it was too soon for his father to introduce James and him to a possible new partner and her family in a new city, the cabin crew appeared with drinks and totally inadequate snacks.

"You've got another forty-five minutes if you want to have a power nap," his father said. "I'm too excited to sleep, and besides, James will never run out of questions. Sure you don't want to swap seats?"

"I have enough unanswered questions of my own, thanks. Can't wait to meet Jenny. She has some of the same questions."

"What? You've talked?"

"Course we have." He quickly added, "And it's all good so far—except for the unanswered questions."

He turned away from his father and pretended to doze.

* * *

James knew this trip was more than visiting an oceanside resort in Nova Scotia. He'd only seen the ocean once, when his parents had taken them to Cuba a couple of years previously. He had preferred playing in the pool, though he had been in the ocean and burned his feet walking up the beach.

His dad had told him the Atlantic Ocean in Nova Scotia, even in the middle of summer, was not warm enough to swim in. The resort had an indoor pool, and James looked forward to that.

What would this Kate woman be like? His father had said she was nice and her daughter, too, and that he would enjoy meeting them both. James wasn't sure. If Kate was around, that meant his dad wouldn't want to come back home. It was strange with his father living in that apartment. James didn't enjoy visiting him there. And it didn't seem right his dad had to phone every time before coming to see them in Kirkland. Even worse, his mom wouldn't invite him over. Mealtimes weren't the same, and whenever Harry and he visited their father, they ate out. It was weird.

Harry didn't like visiting their dad either and had tried to get out of going to their father's apartment the last weekend they'd been there. But he hadn't complained about the weekend away in Nova Scotia. He'd told James it could be a fun trip. James thought it would be better if his mom was flying there with them. And then he remembered that things like that weren't going to happen anymore.

His mother had told him that his father would probably be living with this Kate woman and that this weekend at the resort was a good opportunity for a first meeting. When James had said he wanted to stay in Kirkland and live with her, she had hugged him and said that would happen. "But you'll also be spending time with Dad—and perhaps Kate—on weekends and some holidays. Harry will, too, though he'll be off to college at the end of next summer." She'd hugged him again. "And then it'll just be you and me."

"What about that Aaron person Harry talked about? Don't you like him? Maybe I should meet him if I'm visiting Dad's girlfriend."

"One thing at a time, James. Let's look after you, me, and Harry while things are getting sorted out. Anyways, I already have my two men with you two."

The trouble was that James didn't know what needed sorting or where he would be living when decisions were finally made. He'd asked his father umpteen questions in the airport and on the plane. How could his father have so many "I'm not sure" or "I don't know yet" answers?

James had made it a point to ask all the questions he'd wanted. He learned they could walk on the beach if the weather was not too cold and windy. The five of them would share a three-bedroom chalet, and they would eat in the restaurant. On Sunday, before the flight home, they might spend time in Halifax, which was sort of between the resort and the airport. They would visit the Citadel or the Natural History Museum or the Museum of the Atlantic.

His attention diverted from family problems when the descent into Stanfield International Airport was announced. He wondered what kind of car his father would rent. A van with games consoles, he hoped. Harry might be right. This could be a fun and interesting weekend.

Chapter 49
Chrissie's Quandary

6:30 p.m., Friday, November 27th
19763, rue Sherbrooke, Beaconsfield

When Chrissie's phone rang, she was surprised to see Aaron's number.

"Guess who invited me over for the weekend?"

She almost dropped the phone when he blurted out, "Jill just called!"

And then he continued into his dilemma. He questioned adding to Jill's hurt if he spent the weekend consoling her the only way he knew. For the first time, he seemed to be considering someone else's feelings instead of his own. And Chrissie was dumbfounded when Aaron offered the opinion that sex wasn't really what Jill needed.

"It's too late to back out now, but how do I help her?" He quickly added, "But I don't want to get involved."

Chrissie laughed. "I think you already are, and if you back out after you've agreed to be her consolation—and in the marriage bed, no less—Jill will have nothing left but anger and frustration. Who knows what she might do."

"What do I do?" Desperation tinged his voice.

"You do whatever she wants because she thinks that will take her mind off events in Halifax. But I would bet big bucks that tonight, or sometime this weekend, she will want to talk about Brad, the boys, the Halifax woman, and the breakup and separation and divorce—the whole nine yards."

"Oh shit, how do I deal with that? That's not me."

"I wish it wasn't me, either. But I find myself stuck with similar difficulties too often these days. Listen to Auntie Chrissie's Consolation Quartet."

"What are you talking about?"

"Four unbreakable rules if Jill wants to go beyond drinks, dinner, and naked dessert. Write these down. Number one: Listen! Number two: Stay close! Number three: Only give advice if it's asked for. Most important is number four. If you are expected to say something, be honest, even if it makes you a shit."

When Aaron didn't respond, she asked, "Are you writing these down?"

"Yes, give me a sec." He grunted and moaned, and Chrissie pictured him frantically writing on a notepad.

"Chrissie, what would I do without you? What do I do with this one?"

"Which one do you mean?"

"The one where the lying shit that I am finds himself caring about someone and it scares him to death and—"

"If you're talking about Jill, there's a rule five. Go Slow. She's hurting and fragile and desperate enough to believe anything you say."

"I know all that, and that makes me more afraid of what I'll do or say."

"I have one last piece of advice, and after that you're on your own. The new Sir Aaron is off on his new crusade. And we never had this conversation, did we?"

"Course not! But do you realize you're asking me to multi-task? Men can't do that."

Chrissie assured him he didn't need to write this last one down even though it was something she had wanted to say to countless men since her teen years. She paused and slowly said, "This weekend, Aaron, remember to use your head and your heart instead of that other organ that's guided most of your relationships since you were a teen."

Then she hung up.

Less than fifteen minutes later, the phone rang again. She checked to make sure it wasn't Aaron, which it wasn't. The buzzing continued while she decided whether she wanted to talk to Jill or finish sorting out her outfit for the evening's party. She hoped Jill was calling to play catch-up, not to report on her dinner and "afters" invitation to Aaron.

She finally picked up.

No introductions. "I invited Aaron over for the weekend. What in the hell was I thinking?"

Chrissie cringed. She had to listen to Jill after already listening to Aaron. Jill outlined what she had planned for her and Aaron that evening and most probably the weekend, too. Chrissie quickly clued in that Jill was questioning her decision to invite Aaron as revenge for Brad's weekend dalliance in Halifax.

Be careful what you say, Chrissie warned herself. She let Jill ramble on, almost incoherently, while she gathered her own thoughts. She was beginning to think it would be interesting to stay home and wait for the phone to ring with reports on the Jill and Aaron event, but did she really want to be in the middle of this? How had she gotten herself into a situation where both halves of a couple—and that was using the loosest definition of the term—were seeking her counsel? And neither was aware that the other had sought her advice.

Eventually she jumped in with, "I get the picture, Jill, and I think that you need to do what's good for you."

The monologue from the phone stopped. And then Jill continued with a strangled statement, "But I don't know what to do, Chrissie! What do you think?"

"I think you invited Aaron because you needed somebody. What for and why doesn't matter. You didn't want to be alone this weekend, right?"

Jill agreed. "Once I decided it was either home to Mommy or find a man who would keep me drunk, forgetful, and satisfied, Aaron won on the first ballot. Trouble is, I did a recount after I issued the invitation."

"You went with your instincts and that's probably good. Believe me, moms are seldom consoling in these situations. Been there. It didn't work!"

Both laughed before Chrissie continued. "You know Aaron and how he can distract you. Sounds like a good choice to me. Better the shit you know than some shit picked up in a bar."

She waited for Jill's response, wondering if she could get Jill and Aaron beyond the sexual activities upon which their relationship had been based. *Don't push it, girl,* she cautioned herself, yet again.

"But I do so like him," Jill said, "and not just as a diversion. Trouble is, he never wants to talk about anything. If I try, he either says it's time he left, or he distracts me."

"But this time you have his undivided attention for the whole weekend. Maybe he'll listen if you want to unload."

"Yeah, right! That'll be a first."

"So, what've you got to lose? If he doesn't want to listen and talk about your situation, then he's there for what you invited him for—what can we call it—'forgetful fornication'!"

Chrissie was pleased to hear laughter coming from Jill, which was followed by, "Oh, Chrissie, you take life down to its essentials. If I do get maudlin and want to talk, I'll see how Aaron is. I'm playing at home, so I can always chuck him out if he's not what I want."

"He might just surprise you. He's got to start maturing someday soon. Now I gotta get ready for my big night out. Let me know what happens. And you won't tell Aaron we had this talk, will you?"

"Of course not," Jill said. "Talk later."

I'm getting good at this, Chrissie thought. *If Aaron and Jill get beyond mutually satisfying sex, I'll bottle and sell the advice I just gave them.*

Chapter 50
Jenny's Journey

6:30 p.m., Friday, November 27th
En route to Ash Island Spa and Resort on Nova Scotia's South Shore

Friday evening traffic had lessened by the time Jenny and her mother set out for Ash Island Spa and Resort. The weatherman forecasted a weekend of cold and sunshine. Jenny had neglected to bring a scarf and toque, but she wore a warm jacket though not her heaviest. She hoped she wouldn't need snow boots, not that it mattered. She had every intention of enjoying the indoor comforts of their destination.

The trunk and back seat were crammed with luggage and enough snack foods and beverages to feed every weekend visitor at the resort. Jenny hoped their cabin included a fridge. Being over-organized was becoming one of her mother's less endearing qualities. She seemed to have ignored the fact she was feeding five, not five thousand. Also, she had told Jenny that Brad would be picking up the tab, which included breakfasts and dinners. They would not be going hungry.

With her mother captive in the driver's seat, Jenny took the opportunity to pump her for information. She leaned over to turn off the music. "Mom, is there any more to this weekend than getting Brad's kids and me together?"

"No, of course not." Then she added, "It's an opportunity for Brad and me to be with one another and our children. I think all three of you will like Ash Island. Our cottage is right next to the lodge, close to the pool, lounge, and restaurant. We don't have to be on top of one another like we would in a hotel or, God forbid, our apartment."

As an afterthought, her mother added, "You did remember your swimsuit, didn't you?"

"Yeah, but I'm not sure about wearing the bikini. Might scare Brad and Harry away with that. What about you?"

Her mother laughed. "My bikini days are over, but I'm looking forward to a swim if we can find a time when there aren't too many kids screaming and splashing."

“Good try, Mom. So there isn’t going to be any big announcement by you or Brad? You haven’t decided your kids’ futures and brought us here to drop a bomb on us?”

“Good God, Jenny. Of course not. Their lawyers haven’t even met yet. It’s a long way from being settled. His wife hasn’t given up on reconciliation yet, though Brad has.”

“And both boys know that?”

“They’ve been told, but the younger one is having a hard time. This is just an introductory escape weekend. Next one could be in Montreal, and you know what that means.” Her mother grinned and looked at her.

“Shopping,” Jenny said. “But give me lots of warning so I can save some money. Or maybe Brad will foot the bill for that, too!” She giggled.

“Back off, daughter dear. If Brad is anybody’s sugar daddy, he’s mine.” Her mother pretended to be serious, but Jenny saw through her.

“Thanks, Mom. Now that we have the true nature of your relationship with Brad defined, I can sleep at night.”

“Don’t you dare mention anything like that. It’s all right for you and me to joke, but men never think that’s funny.”

Jenny was relieved there would be no big pronouncements over the weekend.

When her mother exited the highway and veered onto a secondary road, Jenny let her thoughts wander. She looked forward to meeting Harry. Their texts and FaceTime conversations indicated they both searched for definition of the relationship between their father and mother. They hated the state of limbo where nothing could be decided. She feared the longer it went on, the more likely that her mom’s feelings would be diminished by impatience. Her mother was still waiting for her divorce from her father to be finalised. Jenny had an inkling of what her mother was going through and didn’t know if her mother could persevere through the same again—even if it was Brad’s divorce.

Neither she nor Harry had mentioned “divorce.” Nor had she informed Harry of her fears that her mother might not have the strength to handle everything that lawyers and divorce proceedings entailed. Jenny resolved, after this weekend, to raise that topic with her mother.

She slumped in her seat and, as often happened, thought about her father. He’d said that Suzie had gone back to Cape Breton to patch things up with her family. He shared his fear that Suzie was pregnant and that he’d had no opportunity to ask before she left. “I’m so afraid she’ll land on my doorstep, flaunting her baby belly,” he’d said. Jenny cringed at that. Suzie with a baby? Her half-sibling? “That’ll ruin any chances of a new relationship,” her father had added.

Jenny had wanted to shout, "Ya think?" but she didn't. Her father had enough on his mind without her adding to it. But a new relationship? She couldn't believe he had new woman already.

She'd been happy he readily accepted that she wouldn't be with him this weekend as scheduled. Likely he had a heavy date with his "new woman." The next Sunday, Jenny would get to meet his "age-appropriate" woman and her two daughters.

She cast aside her father's problems and concentrated on Harry. She had shared his picture with her friend Cheryl, who had texted back, "He's hot," which made Jenny smile—until her friend's next words, "If he's going to be your brother, he's off limits to you. That makes him all mine!"

"Whoa," Jenny had texted back. "'Let's keep him a secret for now."

Later, when she and Cheryl talked on the phone, Jenny had said she was meeting a potential older brother and baby brother this weekend and two younger sisters the following weekend. Cheryl, the middle of three, said she couldn't imagine going from being an only child to one of five.

Jenny's thoughts drifted back to her father. She hoped he as well as her mother would get into relationships that would be good for them. The thought of Suzie being pregnant triggered a thought that her mother could get pregnant, but she quickly dismissed that idea.

"Here we go," her mother said, bringing her back to the present. "Did you see that? Ash Island Spa and Resort two kilometres away."

Jenny shuddered. Two kilometres away from a meeting place that could radically change her life.

Chapter 51
Jill's Juggling

2:00 a.m., Saturday November 28th
Treetops Terrace, Kirkland, Montreal

Jill eased herself from Aaron's protective arm and his left leg, which was draped across her thigh, and rescued the sheet from the tangle of bedclothes on the floor. The shadows created by the bedside light behind him accentuated his lean and flawless body. With reluctance, she covered it up, realizing she had gotten far more than she had anticipated from him.

After the necessary visit to the bathroom, she poured herself a glass of orange juice and settled into a plush armchair in the den. She should be physically and mentally exhausted. Again, she had ignored the dinner dishes abandoned on the table and the kitchen counter. She and Aaron neglected them in their haste to reach the bedroom. Later, he returned for their wine glasses and the remainder of the second bottle of wine.

She hadn't been surprised at the haste and passion of their after-dinner lust. As practised sexual partners, they knew what the other needed, then and even later, when they relished their togetherness in a more leisurely fashion. She had enjoyed the protracted, pre-midnight sex. Of course, she always had. Maybe her invitation to dinner and "dessert" had been seductive, but who had seduced whom while they undressed each other on the way from the dining room to the king-sized bed?

After they were both sated, a conversation had begun about their relationship beyond the bed. She couldn't recollect who had initiated it, but for some strange reason, she remembered the remark that had taken them in that direction. She told Aaron that he was one of four men she was juggling: him, James, Harry, and Brad. But Aaron, she had told him, was by far the one she most enjoyed.

She had waited for Aaron to fall asleep, which had been his pattern, often triggered by his wish to avoid conversation beyond the erotic. But even with the lateness of the hour and sexual satisfaction, he hadn't drifted off or initiated another round of lovemaking.

Or had he?

While she enjoyed the cold glass of juice, she reflected that the conversation they had enjoyed was different. Coming from Aaron, it had seemed like love.

Love? No! No way!

But right from her opening, Aaron had joined in, acknowledging she had to keep control of her boys but that it was apparent Brad would be a casualty of her juggling.

Jill's response, "I think you're right," was the first acknowledgment to herself that Brad was history, albeit a still-present part of life's negotiations.

Aaron's next question had been the one that surprised her. "Do you want to keep juggling me with the boys, or am I following Brad to the floor?"

She forced a laugh to hide her surprise. "I'm already naked and available in bed, Aaron. You don't have to give me a line to seduce me."

The conversation that followed Aaron's next question was one that Jill hadn't anticipated.

"Are you keeping me as a pretty plaything, or am I becoming too indispensable to drop? And no, Jill, this isn't a line."

"I don't know where you're coming from." She eased gently away so she could see into his face. The pause seemed endless. She scanned her lover's face, knowing he searched for words—a tactic he had long avoided.

"Back in the spring and summer, in those early days, I'd say anything to get you into bed. All that talk about you and Brad being over . . . well, that's all it was to me—talk. And it made you . . ." His eyes gripped hers. "Jill, this is not going to sound good, but let me finish before you hit me."

Jill promised, wondering where he was going with this spiel.

"With you giving up on your husband and marriage, you were easy. Sorry, but that was how I operated with women. And then came bimbo time, when the universities came back and the fall evenings and weekends were full of temptation. I figured I still had a couple of seasons left to compete. Sure enough, one of them threw herself at me, so that gave me an excuse to stop seeing you and what I saw as your 'complications.' And—"

"So, what's different this past month? Are you still playing me?"

Aaron looked down at her. "God knows how many lies and half-truths I've told you. And it's true that when we made contact after you found out about Brad, that I was taking advantage. Behaving as normal, for me. Now I don't know. Things are changing. Maybe I'm changing, or maybe my stories are just getting more sophisticated and I'll never change."

His eyes closed, as if picking his words and checking them twice. "I do know this about us . . ."

For Aaron, it was a long speech, and from someone not used to telling the truth or talking about his feelings or actions, his words came out in a rush. But it was obvious he struggled to find the right words instead of the lies and lines he had exercised for years.

"Once, you were a partner in bed, a sexual conquest. And a very desirable one. You still are. But that's no longer all I want you for. I've gotten to know you and enjoy being with you—and not just while making love."

Another pregnant pause while Aaron again selected his words. "I recognize that you are hurting and that I wasn't helping. But now I want to. And not just in bed."

She freed her arm to gently slap him on the cheek before pulling him close. "That's for saying I'm easy." She kissed him, slithering her tongue in between his lips. Before he could react in his familiar way, she said, "Earlier today I told you that my emotions are all over the place. Well, welcome to the club, Aaron. I don't think that now is the time for us to declare undying love for one another. But I like what I hear, and I want to keep on seeing you. Let's see if we have more than this great sexual connection. Agreed?"

This time the pause was so long she worried she had read him wrong.

But he had pulled her close and whispered, "This is all new to me, Jill. Maybe I'll slip back to my usual selfish self, but right now you are important, and I want you in ways that I can't remember wanting any woman, ever. What we do, where we go, how we continue . . . I need help."

And then he had grasped her close and kissed her. His tongue slithered into her mouth as hers had his.

Half asleep in the recliner, she pulled the throw around her and wondered if it would be the right move to wake him for more meaningful conversation. But the empty juice glass slipped from her hand to the carpet.

Chapter 52
Brightside Brad

6:30 p.m., Saturday, November 28th
Ash Island Spa and Resort lounge bar

Brad took his first gulp of the craft brew the bartender had recommended, relished the hoppy after-taste, and added it to the list of reasons why he looked forward to the move to Nova Scotia. The range and variety of craft beers was a welcome addition to Maritime life.

He sank into the bulky, leather chair facing the roaring log fire in the beach-stone fireplace, the focal point of the lounge. Since he'd picked up the boys more than twenty-four hours previously, this was his first chance to be alone and ponder events of the weekend and the blending of two families. He had been delighted with what he termed "first impressions."

He and the boys had met up with Kate and Jenny, who had already made the common area of their cottage welcoming with snacks on the low table and drinks in the fridge. He hadn't been sure how the three bedrooms would be assigned, but Kate had that figured out. She was a take-charge person, for sure.

Introductions had seemed awkward only to James, who was at the age where any unfamiliar social situation was almost unmanageable. Harry said all the right words to Kate, and he and Jenny were comfortable with each other from the start. Brad guessed that social media connections between the two had helped cement the face-to-face confrontation.

Once introductions were out of the way and the eight o'clock booking for dinner confirmed, Kate showed the boys to their room. Jenny had already claimed the small room with the single bed. Kate carried Brad's tote, almost symbolically, into the third room, where her robe lay, somewhat obviously, on the queen-sized bed.

If Jenny had any qualms about Brad and her mother sharing a bed, they had been resolved before the boys' arrival. The topic wasn't raised to Brad, not even by the ever-questioning James.

Dinner, late for all of them, was eaten too quickly. While Brad and Kate had a final drink in the lounge, Jenny took the boys to show them the pool. Brad and Kate persuaded James that it was too late for a swim at nine-thirty at night, but they promised a swim first thing the next morning. Harry and Jenny also said they'd enjoy the pool. Brad was amused when Kate mentioned Jenny's new bikini and wondered whether she'd wear it in front of Harry. The two seemed too comfortable in each other's company, and Kate was less surprised than Brad that they had been communicating for at least a couple of weeks.

Back at the cottage after dinner, James went to bed while Jenny and Harry retreated to Jenny's room. "Keep the door open," Brad said. He snuck down the hall before he and Kate went to their rooms and saw them on their phones. He hoped they'd be responsible and go to their respective rooms at some point.

He returned to his and Kate's room. For a few minutes, they discussed how great the kids were getting along. Kate said she didn't think Harry was putting on an act and that his charming attitude toward her was genuine. She liked both boys—but would she say otherwise to him?—although conversation with James, she said, was hard work, and dealing with a suspicious, comparing mind didn't make the task easier

While Kate changed into her pajamas and robe, he went into the common area and searched for news on the television. After she entered the room, they announced to the kids that they were going to sleep and would wake them at eight o'clock for breakfast.

"Too early, Dad," Harry yelled. "Tomorrow's Saturday."

Brad overhead him mumble that Kate was a slave driver. And then Jenny shouted, "How about nine, Mom? Harry and I are going to watch a movie."

The only television was in the main area. Brad figured Harry and Jenny would be okay there. Anyone could walk in on them.

"You might as well give up trying to wake Harry early on a weekend," he said to Kate

"Okay then," Kate shouted back. "But don't stay up late."

Brad peeked into the boys' bedroom. James appeared fast asleep. Then he and Kate shut themselves in the bedroom, thankful the television drowned out their conversation and subdued lovemaking.

In the morning, he and Kate emerged to find Harry asleep on the couch. Brad nudged him awake, and he staggered off to his room. Kate started the coffee pot, and then they took advantage of the hot water for a shower.

A half hour later, when Jenny screamed the water for her shower was lukewarm, the three youngsters promised to shower after their swim.

The busy day began once all five had dressed for the chilly walk to the lodge for breakfast. Brad figured the wind would pick up later. After breakfast, at James' urging, they headed across the still-green lawns toward the beach, where the waves crashed against the shore. James ventured too close to water's edge, and an unexpected wave soaked his feet. They all scrambled back to safety, and the final yards were almost a laughing race to the warmth of the cottage.

Brad saw that after-breakfast walk as one of a series of family events that filled the day. He and Kate were focused, not just on each other but on the conversations and interactions that knitted the two families together.

Jenny and Harry took James to the pool. Later, when Brad went to tell them they were driving to a restaurant for lunch and that it was time to get out of the pool, he noticed Jenny wearing a bikini. When he told her the suit looked good on her, Harry shouted, "Careful, Dad. When I told her she was hot, she almost took my head off."

As Jenny sauntered off to dress for the walk back through the November chill, she uttered, "And I thought I was getting a brother, not a sex maniac." Brad wondered if something had gone wrong between her and Harry until he saw the disappearing Jenny glance over her shoulder and grin at them.

Eventually, they crammed into Brad's rental and drove the picturesque coast road to Peggy's Cove. When James wanted to scramble over the rocks toward the pounding ocean, Kate showed him the warning sign at the edge of the carpark, insisting he read it. "One slip on the wet rocks and you'll slide into the water, where you'll disappear forever. It's happened too many times to people, tourists especially, who don't heed the warnings," she said.

Harry made his brother promise to keep close behind him, and they all trekked over the rocks, keeping a safe distance from the crashing waves, before seeking the warmth of the restaurant. Brad announced "No lobster!" and Kate and Jenny grinned. Once seated, Jenny explained about their previous lunch there with Brad.

When James said he didn't understand, Brad delighted in taking him to the tanks where the live lobsters were kept. After they returned to the table, James pronounced, "No lobster for me, either!"

Back at Ash Island, Harry and Jenny took James to the pool. Brad enjoyed the chance to be alone with Kate. He told her the weekend was going well and laughed when she said, "But it's still not real." He argued that it felt like a family spending an active weekend away, to which she responded, "I suppose so."

Unable to get the chill from her bones, Kate said she was going to soak in the tub if there was enough hot water. Brad said he'd check on the kids. After lunch out, they agreed a take-out pizza might be better than a fancy dinner at the resort. He'd confirm that with the kids and then get warm in front of the fireplace.

When Brad appeared at the pool, James got out of the water to join his brother and Jenny on the loungers. All three agreed on pizza, and Jenny suggested a movie everyone could enjoy during and after pizza. Brad left the choice to the kids and promised that drinks and treats would be sufficient for a possible double header.

As he retreated to the lounge to order his drink, he muttered, "How much more family can you get than that?" He congratulated himself on organizing the togetherness weekend, vaguely remembering that Kate had a part in the idea, when Jenny joined him and sat in the opposite chair. "Harry's going in for a last swim before we get James out of the water. Any more time in that pool and he'll be wrinkled all over."

She declined a drink that Brad offered.

"Are you enjoying this weekend?" he asked.

"Of course. I like your boys. Harry and I get along really well. Best of all is that you're giving my mom an opportunity to see what could happen. What it could be like."

He laughed. "That was the idea, Jenny."

"But you have to know my Mom, Brad. She calculates everything. She's so scared of getting hurt again. Did you know her dad left her mom when she was ten? Then she had to get rid of my father because . . . well, cos she had to. So, you gotta be patient with her. Sometimes she won't do things cos she's so cautious."

"And right on cue, here she is," Brad said.

"No hot water again," she said. "I need a seat by the fire." She sat and glanced from him to Jenny. "Are you two talking about me again?"

"You're our favourite subject, but we only say good things about you," Brad said.

"That's nice! And my daughter?"

"She's your biggest fan. And when the youngsters are choosing the movies to go with our pizza, I'll bet Jenny will vote for a chick-flick just for you and her. Right, Jenny?"

"Perhaps," Jenny said.

"I'll ask the bartender where the nearest decent pizza place is. I'll get the phone number and we can order when we want. I'll pick it up."

"Better not choose until the boys get back," Kate said.

Brad smiled. "Do you two have any idea how much I'm enjoying this weekend? Jill and I never did this. This is so . . . so family. So togetherness. You've got to come up to Montreal so we can do the same there."

In unison, Kate and Jenny said, "Slow down, Brad!"

Chapter 53
Kate's Conundrum

4:30 p.m., Sunday, November 29th
Two if By Sea Coffee Bar, Historic Properties, Halifax

Kate cast a worried look in the direction of the door from the Halifax boardwalk. Brad and the boys would be leaving soon for the airport. They hadn't had time to see everything in the Maritime Museum of the Atlantic, but Brad had insisted the boys see the Titanic exhibit. Kate surmised that Jenny, who had visited the museum numerous times, wanted to spend those last minutes alone with Harry.

After a visit to the parade ground of the Citadel to see the noon gun fired, they had made an extended visit to the warmer atmosphere of the Natural History Museum. Kate had declined the third museum in favour of a warming coffee. At the back of her mind was a need to be by herself so she could take stock of the weekend.

The weekend had achieved what she and Brad had hoped. Jenny, Harry, and James spent time together in a neutral environment. They had met their parents' prospective partners and again, on the surface, the introductions had gone well. The boys saw parts of Halifax and enjoyed a weekend at a resort. Jenny had joined in instead of escaping into the depths of social networking. It would be good to get her impressions when they returned home.

While everything had gone well and awkward moments had been minimal and insignificant, Kate wondered why she was feeling apprehensive.

Hers and Brad's relationship would still be a long distance one. A couple of weeks previously, Brad had sneaked down to Halifax, ostensibly for a business meeting. Jenny had visited her father, so Kate and Brad had spent a wonderful evening and night at her apartment. Kate accepted it at face value, but Brad had to keep saying things like, "This is what our life can be like when I move down here." Brad didn't know how to be aware of pitfalls. Maybe he avoided them by making lists of most things that should occur in his life.

It was during this previous visit that Kate cautioned Brad. If Jill persisted in fighting a mud-slinging divorce battle, their relationship would be tested. That night together and the family weekend they were planning were like a honeymoon—the calm before the storm. Kate had been through it once and wondered if she had the strength to go through it again. This last thought she did not share with Brad.

But it was there, buried with other doubts and questions, somewhere in the back of her mind. And it wouldn't go away.

That "something" between her and Brad was still there, reinforced by the uninhibited slow and surreptitious lovemaking on the two nights at the resort. She wondered if Brad evaluated the events they had planned, or did he simply go along without considering what could go wrong, either in the present or the future? His enthusiasm was infectious, and it was easy to go with the flow and not, like she did, wonder what needed to be done to minimise difficulties that were sure to appear.

The door from the harbour boardwalk swung open, and Jenny entered. Kate looked for the others. "I need coffee, Mom. Brad is going for the car and will meet us outside in twenty minutes."

Jenny ordered her coffee and sat across from Kate. "Mom, you're too busy thinking again."

"What? Oh, sorry. So much to think about." She laughed. "It's a good thing for you that I think things through. Living with Miss Impulsivity in the house can be a bad thing."

"I know, but right now it's about you more than me. So far, it all looks good. But if I look too hard, even I can make it all go wrong. Trouble is, you do that too much."

Kate set down her coffee. "Role reversal again, child of mine. It's a mother's job to be cautious, and this mother was never good at just going with the flow."

"Well, give it a try, Mom. That's what this weekend was about."

"I know. And I'm so glad we got through it. And I had no 'what-ifs' until a couple of minutes ago." She had to end the serious conversation. "Bring your coffee. We'd better wait outside for Brad. He's going to drop me off at my car, and I'll follow them to the airport. You coming, or shall I drop you at home?"

"Yeah, I'll go. You should know that, if I have to have brothers, Brad's boys would be good ones to have. Not sure I want Harry as a brother, though. He's cute, and he knows it, too. You should see what my friends said when I posted a picture of us."

"You see why I need to be careful raising you, my not-so-innocent daughter. Now let's go find the others."

They linked arms and headed outdoors.

Chapter 54
Invitations

9:30 p.m., Sunday, November 29th
West Condominiums. Halifax

Kate answered the phone, knowing it would be Brad.

She heard how he had landed safely and taken a cab to his apartment. After this mundane start came the surprise. “Jill met us at the airport, of course, since she wanted to pick up the kids. But guess what?”

Before Kate could answer, Brad finished, “Aaron was with her.”

“What? They’re back together?” Kate was stunned but happy. “More ammunition if and when the divorce gets down and dirty.”

“I think Aaron back in the picture makes things easier. She couldn’t wait to introduce him to us. They’re now an item, and Jill wants the boys to get to know him.”

“How do you know all this?” Kate hoped he hadn’t been talking to Jill.

“Harry called after they got home to see if I was okay and then told me all the news. I guess Jill talked all the way home to Kirkland until Aaron told her to shut up—though not using those words, obviously.”

“He’s okay with all this? Harry, I mean?”

“I don’t know. I assume so. James might have been upset. He asked if Aaron would be living with them ‘because maybe Dad was coming back.’ Harry said he was impressed how Aaron dealt with that. Aaron said he and Jill were good friends and that he’d be visiting often but that I’d always be their father.”

Out of the corner of her eye, she saw Jenny, who was sitting in the armchair, frantically flap her hands as if to say she had information on this development. Kate wondered why and how since her daughter could only hear one side of the phone call.

Kate cut the call short. “Let’s sleep on this. If you find out more, keep me posted. Maybe it is good news. Oh, and Jenny says thank you for the weekend. We both had a good time getting to know the boys.”

“I’ll call after work tomorrow. If Jill doesn’t call to brag about getting Aaron back, I’ll call her. I think this is good for us. And don’t forget to check your schedule, and Jenny's, so the two of you can visit us in Montreal. Love you, Kate."

"Love you, too."

Kate put down the phone, not quite knowing what to make of the call.

"Harry asked me not to tell you, Mom, but he texted to say they'd all met Aaron at the airport and that his mother and Aaron were seeing one another. That is good news, isn't it?"

"Yes, my sweet, optimistic daughter, it probably is. But you don't know the half of what I went through divorcing your father. There's more to come and there's no getting round it. A Jill and Aaron affair is not a miracle. Wish it was."

The phone rang again. "It's Theresa. I'll get rid of her if you want to talk." Almost before Kate had the phone to her ear, Theresa apologized for the late call. She had just gotten off the late shift, and she and the usual suspects were planning another outing for drinks and dinner. "Want to come?"

Once Theresa filled in the details of date, time, and place, Kate squeezed in a response. "Drinks and dinner, maybe, but I'm still recovering from that last stop at Richardson's. I'm not stopping off there again."

"I remember! You got lucky, didn't you? How was it? Anything come of it? Do tell!"

Kate smiled. "Yes, I suppose I did get lucky. It's still going well. He's just got back to Montreal after a weekend here. But you know me, Theresa. What will become of it I'm still not sure."

Jenny hauled herself from the chair, leaned in to Kate, and yelled into the phone, "She's nuts about him, Tessa. And he's lovely!"

"I'll tell you all about it at work tomorrow, Theresa, without my daughter here listening. I'm on for dinner and drinks, but I have to get ready for the morning. And I have to deal with my matchmaking daughter who thinks she's the expert on romance and her mother's affairs."

"Affairs? In the plural? We should finish next Friday at Richardson's and we might all be so lucky," Theresa said.

"Goodbye, Tessa. You're bad."

Kate ended the call and looked at her daughter's questioning gaze, but Jenny was silent.

"That's it, then Jenny. Things to do. And besides, you know all you need to know." Kate paused and reverted to her motherly role. "Maybe you want to talk about you and Harry? A mother needs to know so she can offer advice." She grinned.

Her daughter stuck out her tongue and said, "He has a girlfriend. Lynsey. He's cute, but . . . Brotherly love is the only possibility there. Too bad! Now, unless you want to give me a note saying I couldn't do my assignment cos we spent the weekend with your boyfriend, I have homework to finish."

The cushion Kate threw at her daughter hit the door that closed behind her. Kate reached for the Pinot Grigio, convincing herself that another glass of celebratory wine was called for.

She reflected, gazing at the wineglass glowing in the half light. Her thoughts drifted to a time she had worked with confused adolescent patients at the children's hospital. The psychiatric assessment of the more difficult situations sometimes contained "GOK" as a prognosis for the teens' future.

God Only Knows! And, she speculated, even with all that had transpired, that was the prediction for her romantic future.

But she smiled anyway.

AFTERWORD

Many who write for the sheer satisfaction to be earned from this creative form believe they have a novel inside them. The writer pretends to be awaiting an inspirational stimulus, along with time and opportunity to unleash it. I have held to this belief for forty years since I started to enjoy my hobby. I was forty when that happened and in my eightieth year, decided it was now or never for my novel.

My reading preferences of history or mystery should have led me to one of those genres. My writing record has been short stories, pieces for children I had taught, over-involved poetry, and personal writing. None of these inspired an extended novel.

A first prize for *Am I Dreaming*, judged the best novel for children in the Atlantic Writing Competition of the Writers' Federation of Nova Scotia (WFNS) in 1991, kept me striving to write productively. Twenty years later, the publication of short stories and my memoir have kept me stimulated.

Perhaps I was merely dreaming about a novel until I wrote a short romantic story inspired by a prompt offered to our Evergreen Writers Group. The story morphed into an opening chapter of a novel. But could a man, in his eightieth year, compose a romance that would have appeal for those who enjoy this genre? Did I have the inspiration and perseverance to complete the work and find an audience?

Like the connected characters in my novel, I will have to "wait and see."

Tom Robson

ABOUT THE AUTHOR

Tom started to write in his forties when his target audiences were the elementary students he taught. Flushed with two successes in Atlantic writing contests, he continued this into retirement. Writing was a hobby, purely for enjoyment, until he had three ghost stories published in *Out of the Mist*, an anthology compiled by the Evergreen Writers Group. His adaptation into a performance piece of Catherine Scholes' book *Peace Begins with You* is in *The Peaceful School: Models That Work* by Hetty Van Gurp.

A collection of stories and poems, some true, some depending on artistic licence and selective memory, were written over a thirty-year period. They have been assembled into *Written While I Still Remember: A Patchwork Memoir*, published in 2014 by Mackenzie Publishing.

He enjoys writing short stories and journals of his travels. He occasionally tries to be poetic and wants to gather his poems from the depths of his computer for publication. This will have to wait until he proves that it is possible for a man in his eightieth year to write a successful romantic novel.

Tom was born a proud Yorkshireman and enjoyed his youth in the New Forest where he first became a teacher. He came to Canada in 1971. He now lives with his wife in Halifax, Nova Scotia.

SOCIAL MEDIA LINKS

Contact Tom at:
trobson@accesswave.ca

Wait and See Facebook Page:
(Wait and See Book)
https://www.facebook.com/Wait-and-See-Book-816844611823367/

Like Tom on Facebook:
https://www.facebook.com/tom.robson.545

Tom's Blog:
Robson's Writings
www.robsonswritings.wordpress.com

***

Available on Amazon (print and e-book):

Written While I Still Remember:
A Patchwork Memoir

Out of the Mist:
22 Atlantic Canadian Ghost Stories
(an anthology by the Evergreen Writers Group)

www.ingramcontent.com/pod-product-compliance
Lightning Source LLC
Chambersburg PA
CBHW060929180626
46817CB00004B/1460
* 9 7 8 1 9 2 7 5 2 9 4 9 2 *